DEADLY

Luke
The chai
ring of c
from a
between
ajar, but

"John!

No rep
movement back in the cell area.

"John?"

Dewitt, who had entered the office behind Luke, said quietly, "He ain't going to answer you, Luke."

"Where is he, Dewitt?"

Dewitt's eyes cut toward the door leading from the office into the cellblock area.

Luke knew intuitively what he would find when he opened that door. But he was the marshal. He had to do it.

He went to the cellblock door and pulled it open.

Now he knew what had become of John Bailey.

Other *Leisure* books by Cameron Judd:

MR. LITTLEJOHN
CAINE'S TRAIL
THE TREASURE OF JERICHO MOUNTAIN
BAD NIGHT AT DRY CREEK
BEGGAR'S GULCH

CAMERON JUDD

Outlaw Train

LEISURE BOOKS NEW YORK CITY

A LEISURE BOOK®

March 2010

Published by

Dorchester Publishing Co., Inc.
200 Madison Avenue
New York, NY 10016

ISBN 10: 0-8439-6398-0
ISBN 13: 978-0-8439-6398-4
E-ISBN: 978-1-4285-0863-7

Visit us online at www.dorchesterpub.com.

Outlaw Train

PROLOGUE

Bug Otis looked past Ben Keely toward an obese man who sat in the far corner sloppily eating from a bowl of potatoes, beef, carrots, and onions. "Dry stew," the proprietor of the place called that particular dish, the specialty of this dank and dirty dining establishment in the backwoods of western Kentucky. Most days, including this one, it was the only dish served.

Bug, a very skinny man with leathery, furrowed skin and bulging eyes that accounted for his nickname, swiped a filthy sleeve across his mouth and sighed.

"Lordy, Lordy," he said. "I'm just like my old daddy, I reckon."

"How so, Bug?" Keely asked. "I remember your father well, and you ain't like him at all. You're your mother all over again."

"Yeah, but my old daddy, he always said it made him hungry to watch a fat man eat. And I'm the same way."

Keely looked back over his shoulder toward the man Otis was watching. He turned back again, amazed and repelled. "Bug, are you trying to tell me it makes you hungry to watch that big old boar back there slopping himself?"

Bug frowned. "Well . . . yeah. Don't it you?"

"You're a sick man, Bug. Sick in the mind. Loco, as the Mexicans say it." Keely tapped a finger against his temple.

Bug looked annoyed. "We're all different, I reckon, but that don't mean I'm crazy. Hell, Ben, me and you been different since we was boys."

Ben Keely took a bite of corn bread and didn't reply. But Bug was right. Ben always had been different from not only Bug, but most of the folks he'd grown up among. Didn't think like them, act like them, want to be part of them for longer than he had to. Which, he supposed, was part of what had driven him away from home so early. He'd gone west when he left Kentucky, because that was the direction a man went in the post–Civil War United States of America if he wanted to get to something new and better and bigger. Always west. Ben had crossed the Mississippi with no firm plan to ever make a return trip. And until the death of his father two weeks back, he'd not done so. Once free of Kentucky, he'd settled and stayed in the little town of Wiles, Kansas, hiring on as town marshal (nobody else had wanted the job, and he'd been willing to lie about his credentials) and trying to forget his past.

Not that he'd had a bad life growing up. Good parents, intelligent, his father a schoolmaster and devotee of history, his mother educated as well. They'd raised him and his sister, Bess, with a respect for learning, a tolerance for difference, and a belief that they could rise above their narrow little backwoods world. The world is big, Ben's father used to tell his children. Don't let anybody keep you small in a world this big.

Ben had left home at age seventeen, hoping that big world his father talked about really was out there, and had wandered about for years looking for it. Sometimes he believed he'd found it, but most times had to admit that life as a town marshal in a little railroad stop Kansas town was not much bigger or better than the life he'd left behind in Kentucky. A more open landscape, certainly, a broader view and more distant horizon . . . but the world right at hand, the streets he trod while making his rounds, the saloons he dragged rowdy drunks from, and the simple little jailhouse where he kept his meager office and locked up his prisoners, these were as small and strangling as anything he'd left behind in Kentucky.

Ben was distressed when he pondered that he was living a mostly solitary life at a time when his youth was beginning to pass away. Before he knew it, he'd be halfway through his thirties, still unmarried, still tied down to an unproductive and unpromising job he'd intended to keep only for months, not years.

Ben refocused his attention on his food, trying not to hear the disgusting mashing and gulping noises made by the obese eater in the corner. For his part, Bug couldn't resist staring hungrily at the hideous spectacle. Each round of observation brought him back to his own bowl of beef, potatoes, and onions with invigorated appetite.

Ben picked at his food and tried not to feel queasy. Bug finished his victuals, wiped his forefinger around the bowl, and noisily sucked the finger clean. With that, Ben's appetite died fully and he simply stared into the remnants of his food.

"You ain't going to finish that?" Bug asked.

Ben shoved his bowl across the table. Bug's eyes were all but bulging out of his skull. "You letting me have this?"

"Enjoy it, Bug. I've had my fill."

At that moment the outer door opened, spilling murky sunlight into the dim interior of the log building from the drizzly, gray day outside. The muted backlighting allowed Ben a relatively clear view of the unusual man who entered.

He was clad in loose brown trousers that were tucked into high boots. Not the cattleman's boots Ben saw so frequently in Kansas, but moccasin-styled boots that were strapped to the calves, nearly to his knees, canvas trouser legs plunging into them. His shirt was big and loose and made out of highly worked supple leather, styled like an old hunting shirt. The man's face was smoothly shaven and had an olive tone that might have been Indian, Egyptian, or Mediterranean. Hard to judge in the light.

Oddest of all, the man wore a turban. Ben had seen pictures of turbans before in some of his father's history and geography books that showed images from the Far East and the biblical lands, and he knew similar headgear had been worn by Indians in the region years earlier, and in times past by older slaves farther south. Ben did not know which kind of turban he was seeing here. Whatever it was, it was nothing he would have expected to encounter in rural Kentucky.

Bug noticed Ben's distraction and turned to investigate. He gave a soft grunt. "Huh! Man's got a rag tied around his head! And look there at his ears."

Bug had noticed something Ben had missed. The edges of the stranger's ears were discolored . . . blue. Tatooed, Ben decided. But the door closed, the light became as dim as before, and he couldn't see clearly enough to verify it.

"Wonder who that is?" Bug said a little too loudly. Ben wished he hadn't. He had an inexplicable bad feeling about the new arrival and didn't want to draw his attention. Too late. The stranger heard Bug and looked in their direction.

But he didn't approach. He found a table close to the door and sat down. Mutton Smith, who ran this establishment, came around and informed the stranger that the only item on the menu today was dry stew, but by gum, if you had dry stew available, what else could you want anyway? The man nodded to confirm his order. One more dry stew coming up.

At that moment, Bug stretched his legs and accidentally kicked over a closed crockery jar that sat under the table near Ben's feet. It clunked and rolled. Ben bent to the side and quickly grabbed it, setting it on the tabletop.

"I be damned, Ben!" Bug exclaimed loudly, staring at the jar. "That's the Harpe head jar, ain't it! I didn't know you had brung that with you!"

At Bug's words, the man in the turban suddenly turned his full attention toward Ben and Bug's table.

"Ain't no call to tell the whole world about it, Bug," Ben said, noticing and not liking the stare he was getting from the turbaned man. Something unnerving in it. "Keep your voice down, would you?"

Bug answered as loudly as before. "Hell, Ben, that there jar of bone ain't no secret around here! Everybody knows that the Keely family has Harpe's head! That's been printed in newspapers before! I ain't saying nothing everybody don't already know."

The man in the turban rose and walked toward their table. Ben tensed and put his hand on the jar, at which the man's dark eyes were staring. It roused in Ben a strangely intense protectiveness toward his possession. This was a family heirloom, something his father had prized for its historical value and closely guarded all his life. The contents of the jar were unique and irreplaceable, and if they had no inherent monetary value, they were of value as a relic.

The turbaned man reached the table. Ben and Bug looked up at him, silent and unwelcoming. Bug studied the newcomer as if he were an oddity, a man with three heads or four eyes.

"Can I help you, mister?" Ben asked.

The man smiled broadly and thrust out his hand, which Ben for the moment ignored. "You may call me Raintree, sir. Professor Percival Raintree, collector and showman who travels these great United States. You, I'm guessing, are Mr. Keely?"

That took Ben aback. How could this odd stranger know him?

"Why do you think my name's Keely, stranger?"

"Because of that crockery jar, sir. I heard your

companion here refer to the Harpe's head jar, and I have studied the lore sufficiently to know that the head of Big Harpe has for many years been a possession of the Keely family of this district of Kentucky. And given your age and the fact that it is no surprise that you would have come home because of the death of your father—my condolences, by the way—it was easy to surmise that you could hardly be anyone else than the remaining son of the Keely family, Mr. Ben Keely, late of this district and now, I'm told, a man of the law in Kansas. Kansas . . . a state I hope to visit soon, with my traveling show."

Ben took a quick breath. "You've studied my family a good deal, it seems."

"Only as a sideline to my main area of interest, sir: the lore of the criminals that have made themselves infamous in our great nation. My interest in your family relates solely to your family's possession of that famous skull." He paused and looked closely at the crockery jar. "May I, sir?"

"Sit down first. I don't want you in a position to get this jar in hand and then run out the door with it."

Raintree pulled over a chair and sat down, never taking his hungry eyes off the crockery jar. "Is the entire skull still in there?"

"It is, as best I know, though of course it is mere dust and fragments now," Ben replied, wondering why he was even talking to this odd stranger. "It was dust and fragments before it went into the jar to begin with."

Raintree spoke. "Amazing story, that of the Harpes.

Amazing and terrible. No worse murderers have lived or died. And given the cruelty of his life, it is no surprise that Micajah Harpe's own killer chose to behead him, and put that head on display in a tree as a symbol of justice and warning to other evil men."

"Yep," Bug said, entering the conversation. "And then when that head rotted down to the bone, a witch woman took it out of that tree and ground it up to do magic with, and put it in that there jar. But she never got around to using the bone. Just kept it."

"And the Keely family later purchased it," Raintree rejoined. "Setting a precedent for what I have come to Kentucky to do."

"What do you mean?" Ben asked.

Raintree paused and seemed to be collecting his words. "Mr. Keely, I must believe it is fate that brought me to this . . . this fine establishment today. For it is to find the Keely family, and their famous jar of bone, that I came to Kentucky. How I would find you, I didn't fully know, but now I have literally stumbled upon you, the man I seek, bearing the very relic I seek. Fate is at work. I want to buy that jar of bone from you, Benjamin Keely."

The conversation was interrupted by the arrival of Raintree's wooden trencher of dry stew. He accepted it in a distracted manner. He was taking a bite of the tough, chunky beef when a loud, resounding belch came from the corner where sat the fat diner who had inflamed Bug's appetite. Raintree looked up, disgust on his face, and let a second bit of meat fall back into his trencher.

"I seem to be losing my appetite," he said.

"If you don't want that food, I'll take it," Bug said, but Raintree either ignored or didn't hear him.

"The Harpe's head jar ain't for sale, Mr. Raintree," Ben said. "It's part of my inheritance. My parents weren't rich folk by any stretch. They had little of money value to leave me and my sister, but they left us what they could, including an appreciation for heritage, for history. And that's what that jar is to me: history. An ugly part of history, no question about it. But it was my father's possession, and now it's mine."

"But there is a price for all things, sir. Surely there is one for a mere jar of bone." He sighed and looked thoughtful. "A shame that mere dust is all that remains. Imagine how grand a relic it could have been had there been a way to preserve the head whole! And it could have been done. I know a man who could have turned that head into a trophy that would last for many, many years."

Ben found the line of conversation strange and off-putting. "Mr. Raintree, I have nothing to sell you. And that's more than a 'mere jar of bone.' That's the bone of one of the wickedest devils ever to wear human flesh. And it's something I inherited from a father I'll never see again. Now please, eat your food and leave me alone."

Raintree's eyes flared, a sudden anger that made him look dangerous. Ben inadvertently drew back. The atmosphere crackled with tension, but then suddenly the fat man in the corner belched again, a massive eructation, and Ben had to chuckle. The tension was broken.

Raintree took a bite, seemed to find it acceptable,

and ate in silence for two minutes, staring at the jar. He swallowed another bite, pulled a handkerchief from his pocket, and dabbed at the corner of his mouth. "Mr. Keely, sir, you seemed to indicate a moment ago that, if I would sit, you might let me hold that jar."

Ben shook his head. Raintree was openly disappointed.

"C'mon, Ben," Bug said. "He seems a good feller. Let him hold it. You've let other folks hold it before. You even let me look inside at the bones once, remember?"

Raintree's face lit with hope.

"We were boys then, Bug. I opened that jar on the sneak, without Pa knowing, 'cause you wouldn't leave me alone about it." Ben paused. "You ain't changed much by growing up, Bug. Still a pest and bother."

"Let him see it, Ben," Bug urged.

Ben's temper got the best of him, but he kept his voice low and steady. "No, Bug. I don't trust him. He's a stranger and he's dressed like a wise man on the way to see baby Jesus. A little too odd to suit me. No offense, Mr. Raintree. Just speaking the truth. If you want to ask favors of folks, you might want to present yourself in a way that ain't so . . . so different."

"I promise you, sir, I will not attempt to flee this place with that jar. I merely want to make you an offer, a cash offer, for its purchase. I wish to add this relic to my collection . . . a collection I show as a traveling display for the entertainment and education of the people of our great nation, and for my own living. As for my 'different' manner and look . . . I am a showman. It is my profession, my livelihood. It is to my advantage to be 'different.' Difference is memorable. It catches the eye and rouses the interest."

"Back to the point: the jar of bone dust ain't for sale."

"Be reasonable, sir."

"This jar is my inheritance from my father, odd as it may be. I came all the way from Kansas to bid my farewells to him at his graveside, and now I'm taking this one last piece of his life back to Kansas with me."

Something in Raintree's face changed, darkened. He made a little snarling motion with his lip and concentrated on his eating, talking no further to Ben Keely.

Bug was still talkative. "Mister, if you're wanting to show Big Harpe's skull dust in a jar, hell, you could just throw some old cow bone in a jar of your own and tell folks that's what it is! They'd never know."

Raintree lifted one brow. "I admit that there have been times I have lowered myself to, er, slight deceptions for the sake of showmanship, but I am loath to fake a relic if the real thing is available and at hand, as is this one."

Ben had no interest in this argument. He stood. "Good day, gentlemen." He tucked the Harpe head jar under his right arm and left unceremoniously, having paid Mutton Smith for his meal in advance.

"If it was me, I'd have sold it to you," Bug said to Raintree.

"Oh, Mr. Keely may sell it to me yet. He and I have

not finished our negotiations," Raintree returned. "I believe our next conversation will put him in a much more accommodating frame of mind."

"I don't know. He's a stubborn one, always has been."

Raintree smiled. "And with the stubborn, sometimes the solution is to adjust the mode of persuasion. And I can be a persuasive man."

"Well, don't take too long. He's planning to head back toward Kansas later today. Riding out on the afternoon train."

Raintree rose, pulled money from his pocket and left it beside his plate, and was gone.

Bug pulled Raintree's plate toward him and ate the remnants of his food. He slyly sneaked the money Raintree had left and slid it under the edge of his own bowl, putting Raintree's now fully emptied trencher back where it had been.

As Bug rose, he looked back toward the rear, where the crude kitchen was, and hollered back at Mutton Smith, "That feller with the cloth 'round his head, he left without paying you! 'Ja hear me, Mutton?"

Then Bug vacated the place as quickly as he could.

The fat diner in the corner did not betray Bug's trickery. He had fallen sound asleep and was snoring loudly, oblivious of all.

Ben Keely all but forgot about the odd encounter in Mutton Smith's place before he'd ridden three miles. Just killing time now until it was time to go to the train station. The Harpe's head crockery jar was safely ensconced in a bulging saddlebag and Keely's mind was drifting, pondering the situation in which he found himself these days.

Odd, he pondered, how a family as close as his own had been had managed to become estranged. It was sad, but he couldn't see how things could have gone much differently. His parents had been so devoted to each other and to the life of the mind that they shared, a life utterly different than the great majority of lives lived around them, that they'd paid only limited attention to their children. Ben and Bess Keely had grown up guided and shaped mostly by their own inclinations and natures, going their individual ways. Ben's path had been a westward journey and a quest for independence; Bess's path had not led her away from Kentucky geographically, but she'd gained a reputation. She was a young woman who tended to draw attention, and there had been many whispers about her, crude and impolite rumors, things Ben did not want to believe, and tried to dismiss. When he'd left home and headed west, he'd simply chosen to try to forget about such things.

Then had come the recent news from Bess of the death of their father. Their mother had passed on years earlier, so Ben and Bess were now orphans, albeit grown ones. Ben had pondered the possibility of ignoring the message and not returning to Kentucky. His father was already dead and buried, after all, his mother was long gone, and there was nothing much to be gained by a homecoming.

But for the sake of improving his relationship with his sister and in hope of finding at least some tangible token of his past to take back to Kansas with him, he had come home. The matter of his sister had not worked out as hoped. They were more estranged even than they had been before. But he had gained the token: this jar of crumbled, dusty bone that had been the skull of Micajah "Big" Harpe, the murderer who had been beheaded at the close of the previous century.

Ben wondered why that jar of bone mattered so much to him. Of all things a man could cling to as a memory of his father, could he have made a stranger choice?

He dismissed the question and told himself the choice made perfect sense. His father had been such a devotee of history and antiquities that he had considered the Harpe's head jar a treasure of great significance. He'd more than once noted that a man rarely is privileged to hold history in his own hands, and should treasure that chance when it comes. Even if the piece of history being held is one most would as soon forget.

Of course, there were those odd types, such as that turbaned fellow in Mutton Smith's place, who seemed to have an interest in such things that was vaguely different. Unhealthful. Ben disliked the notion of putting his father's prized relic on public display for the price of admission to some traveling chamber of mysteries. In a legitimate and scholarly museum, maybe. A cheap crime carnival, no.

Ben halted his horse, dismounted, and went to the side of the road to relieve himself. He was heading back to mount up again when he heard movement in the woods nearby, and the faint but unmistakable click of a firearm hammer being thumbed back. A shotgun, if Ben had to guess.

Turning, Ben spoke to the woods behind him. "Bess, is that you out there?"

No answer.

"Bess, has it really gotten that ill between us? Has it actually come to *this*?"

Still no reply.

"Bess, is it you? Bess?"

"Is that who I am?" a voice returned.

"Good God!" Ben whispered.

He knew when he heard the voice what was about to happen.

PART ONE
WILES, KANSAS

CHAPTER ONE

Jimmy Wills was tired. He worked as night clerk at the Gable House Hotel, the only hotel in the town of Wiles, Kansas, and he'd been awake all night. And it wasn't over yet, even though morning had come and the usual hour of his release was at hand. But Jimmy had agreed to fill in for the day clerk as well, that clerk being waylaid by sickness. It had been easy to agree to the extra duty when he considered the prospect of additional pay. Now, though, he longed for his bed and pillow. Oh well. He'd get there eventually. His volunteering for the upcoming day shift would free him from the next round of night duty. If Jimmy could make it through this day, come the next nightfall he'd have the rare privilege of sleeping when it was dark, just like normal folk who didn't have to stay up nights staring at an empty hotel lobby and waiting for late-arriving customers.

Last night had been busy, in an odd way. Throughout the night, men had entered the lobby, four total, one at a time, each acting strangely, looking around as if the hotel were full of spying eyes. Then each had waited until Jimmy's back was turned and slipped up the stairs to the third floor like a bad little boy sneaking into the pantry for the cookie jar.

Jimmy could easily figure out what was going on, and who and what was at the center of it. Mr. Gable would probably drop over dead from shame when he learned what use the top floor of his hotel apparently was being put to.

A loud thump startled Jimmy and drew his attention to the only other person in the lobby, a thin, worn-looking local fellow named Dewitt Stamps. Stamps had dropped the heavy book he'd been reading quietly in one of the plush chairs scattered around the lobby. He'd slipped in just as the sun was beginning to rise.

"Whatcha reading there, Dewitt?" Jimmy asked.

"Same thing I always read," Stamps replied. "Only book worth reading."

"You ain't read that Bible through yet?" asked Jimmy. "As much time as you put to it, seems like you'd be through it two or three times by now."

"It's a mighty long book, Jimmy, and I read slow. And I take time to think about it. You read the Bible?"

"Can't say I do," Jimmy said. "Heard it read some, though. In church and Sunday school."

"You ought to read it for yourself," Stamps said. "Everybody should."

"I ain't much for reading. A few yaller novels from time to time is about it for me."

"Well, you ought to read your Bible. It'll change your life. Look at me, if you don't believe it!"

Jimmy couldn't argue with that. Dewitt Stamps indeed was a much-changed man since the religious conversion that had made him the talk of the town four years earlier. Dewitt had spent much of his adult life as the town drunk of Wiles, Kansas. Shunned and scorned by the righteous church folk, he'd been much loved by his fellow residents of the town's underbelly because of his innately generous nature. When he had liquor, he shared it. Now that he had religion, he was eager to share that as well, so his former drinking cohorts fled his presence like demons before an exorcist.

Jimmy left his place behind the front desk and walked over near Dewitt.

"I have to admit, Dewitt, you really aren't the man you used to be. You remember when Mr. Gable was always throwing you out of this very lobby because you'd be in here drunk? Sometimes even this time of morning? And now you're sober as a judge every day, and instead of staggering in here to pass out, you're in here reading your Bible. Different world, huh, Dewitt?"

"Grace of God, Jimmy. Grace of God."

Just then a woman in a pale red dress stepped onto the landing of the staircase overlooking the lobby, catching the eyes of the two males.

The woman's name, at least according to the hotel register she had signed, was Katrina Haus. She was remarkably pretty and buxom, and Jimmy could not tear his eyes away from her bosom, the size of which was emphasized by its contrast with her slender waist.

Jimmy tried not to stare, not wanting to offend the woman, but when he remembered the men who had climbed the stairs to her floor during the night, he decided she was unlikely to take offense simply at being stared at. Her dress obviously was designed to emphasize her feminine attributes. Katrina Haus was a woman who sought to attract stares, not turn them away.

But when Jimmy glanced back over at Dewitt, Dewitt wasn't staring at her. His eyes were fixed downward, on the big, weather-beaten Bible that was his constant companion for the past few years. Stamps seemed tense, nervous. Only when Katrina Haus was out of the hotel and the door had closed behind her did he relax and let out a slow, long breath.

"Son, that there was a powerful temptation. Lust-of-the-eyes kind of temptation," Dewitt said.

"Yes, sir, and I gave in to it something fierce," Jimmy said, grinning. Dewitt was not amused. He looked seriously at the younger man.

"You ought not joke about that which can damn a man's soul," Stamps lectured. "Jesus hisself said that to look on a woman with lust is the same as committing adultery with her. I can show you right here in this Bible where he said that."

"Don't bother . . . I've heard it before. And that's why I can't ever be like you and get religion down to the bone, Dewitt. It's just too hard. Too much to give up. And hell, it just don't make good common sense to me that a man would be damned just for being a man. Just for seeing a pretty woman and enjoying it."

"God's law may not make sense to you, Jimmy, but it's God's law all the same. Break it and you die. But you can swap death for life. That's the exchange I made."

"Yeah . . . well, you were drinking yourself into the grave. Me, I got no big sins like that to repent from. I'm just a regular, normal, little-sins kind of gent. And you can preach about lust and such all you want, Dewitt, but there ain't no normal man alive who can see what come down those stairs just now and not think sinful thoughts. I mean . . ." He cupped his hands over his chest and moved them up and down. "Did you *see* them things? Each one of them hanging off her all big and bouncy . . . wouldn't you like to just reach out to them and—"

Dewitt looked distressed and shook his head. "You shut up that kind of talk, Jimmy! You're making me think about things I oughtn't think about!"

Jimmy grinned wickedly and moved his cupped hands more vigorously out about a foot from his chest. "Bounce, bounce, bounce . . ."

"They warn't *that* big, Jimmy!"

Jimmy had Dewitt where he wanted him. "Listen to you, Dewitt! Talking about women's bosoms . . . you think the Lord would like you doing that?"

Dewitt shoved a pointing finger into Jimmy's face and shook it. "You mock me like that and I'll slap you down, boy! I'll be on you like Jesus on a money changer!"

Jimmy laughed in scorn. "You're a good Christian man. Right, Dewitt? That means you got to love and forgive me. None of this threatening and such!"

"But you're trying to lead me into sin! Making me talk indecent, making me think about wrong things, making me get all mad and ready to fight . . ."

Jimmy chuckled. "You got to calm down, Dewitt. You're way too wrought up over religion. Don't take me wrong . . . I'm glad you gave up the liquor and got yourself forgave and heaven-bound and all that.

But a man has to keep his perspective, keep things in good order and balance. The way I figure it, if God made men to like the beauty of a fine woman, and then made a woman like the one who just passed through here, well, hell, he must have meant for a man to look at her and 'preciate her."

"Ain't what the holy word says, Jimmy, much as you might like it to be. And you ought not be cussing when you talk about the Lord. Besides, I don't think lusting and 'preciating are the same thing."

Jimmy sighed and spoke more softly. "Don't you ever miss your old life, Dewitt? I mean, I know the liquor near done you in, cost you your wife and family, and made you a poor man . . . but don't you ever wish you could have you some fun like you used to do before you gave it all up? I reckon religion is a fine thing, and it's done you a world of good, but you ain't as fun as you once was. You just ain't. No drinking, no looking at women no matter how big their bosoms is, much less funning with them . . . don't you ever miss none of that, Dewitt?"

Dewitt suddenly seemed to be having trouble with his voice. It was hard for him to get his words out. "Jimmy, I'm still a man. I'm tempted just like anybody. The book says Jesus hisself was tempted. It ain't no sin to be tempted, Jimmy. Just when you give in to it . . . that's where the sin comes in."

"Clear your throat, Dewitt. You sound shaky."

"Jimmy, I can't listen to you no more. You want to see me go the wrong way. You want to turn me off the straight and narrow path."

Jimmy frowned and seemed to be weighing something in his mind. He suddenly clapped Dewitt on the shoulder and said, "Dewitt, come over here with me a minute."

Looking doubtful, Dewitt followed Jimmy back to the front desk near the entrance. Jimmy went behind the desk, stooped and reached inside, and came back up with a bottle and glass in hand. A whiskey bottle, half-full.

Dewitt gaped. "Jimmy, why you getting *that* out? I don't even want to see that stuff no more. And if you're getting that out for yourself, you're heading down a road you don't want to be on. I can tell you that from the life I've lived."

Jimmy took a slow breath, pulled the cork on the bottle, and poured a generous shot into the glass, which he picked up, examined against the light of the window, and held toward Dewitt.

Dewitt looked aghast. "What the hell are you . . . now, see? You've even got me to cussing again! And I ain't cussed in three years!"

"Dewitt, I'm trying to help you, not hurt you. And I think you'd help yourself if you'd lighten your own burden a little. Since you got religion, you been trying to be a perfect man. And you can't. Nobody can. You'd be better off if you'd shoot for a little lower target. You can give up being a drunk without giving up every drop of liquor. You can give up sinning with women without having to strike yourself blind and pretend a pretty woman ain't a pretty woman."

Dewitt shook his head firmly. "That might be true for you and a lot of others, but it ain't true for me. For me, if I was to take that one glass of whiskey, I might as well jump into a pond full of the stuff. It's like a sickness with me, Jimmy. You ought to know that. You're young, but not so young as to not understand what it is to be trapped in a bottle like I was for so long. Put that glass away, and that bottle. I don't want them."

"But you do. I can see that you do."

"Same way a rat wants its poison."

Jimmy cursed in frustration, put the bottle back under the desk, then marched with the shot glass to the door. Opening the door, he tossed the whiskey out onto the porch and came back inside.

"I just poured out good whiskey, Dewitt. Damned waste. If I shouldn't have been offering that to you, then I'm sorry. But here's the point I was trying to make: there's more to life than following rules and living for some notion of religion that demands more of you than anybody can give. Relax a little, Dewitt. Don't let yourself forget how to enjoy life in this world while you're aiming for the next one."

"Jimmy, I think you're trying to tell me what you think is good for me to hear. But it ain't the same for me as it is for most people. I drank too much of my life away. Too much of my soul. I can't never touch a drop again in my life. Not a drop. That's all it would take to drown me, Jimmy. Just one drop of whiskey. One little drop. As for pretty women, Jesus hisself said you was adulterizing yourself just to lust after one."

It was Jimmy's turn to shrug. "I'll take your word for it, Dewitt. But if you can't take my advice on everything, at least listen to this: don't be so preachy at folks. It don't draw them to you and your religion. It puts them off. Pushes them away."

"I can't hide my light under a bushel, Jimmy." Dewitt put his Bible under his arm and headed for the door. "I'll be seeing you around. I hope you see the light someday." He headed out to the street.

CHAPTER TWO

Luke Cable, deputy and acting marshal of the town of Wiles, Kansas, was doing his best to look interested in the conversation in which he was engaged on the porch of the Wiles Dress and Fabric Shop, located across the street from the Gable House Hotel.

"And as I've made clear, Marshal, I do not hold you at fault that you cannot keep a perfect restraint upon all the undesirable elements in this town," said Clara Ashworth, leading citizen and staunchest female member of the Wiles Presbyterian Church. She had initiated the conversation by showing off the box of new pearl-headed, French-made hat pins she'd bought earlier at the dress shop. DIRECT FROM PARIS, the foot-long hat-pin box declared of its contents. Then the conversation had taken a less frivolous turn as she began discussion of Luke's job performance. "No one man could be expected to achieve that high a goal, especially one such as yourself, who lacks the age and experience to prevail over the criminal aspects of our town."

"I'm sorry you find I'm doing so poor a job," Luke mumbled, eyes darting, looking for any pretext for escape.

"I think you've done quite well, under the circumstances, abandoned as you were by your superior."

Luke found no response. The woman had just voiced a statement he'd made in his own mind many times, usually in a mood of mounting resentment toward Ben Keely, the town marshal who had left him in charge of Wiles law enforcement while Ben himself left for Kentucky to pay his last respects to his late father.

Movement on the hotel porch across the street caught Luke's eye. For the first time in his life he had the experience of being glad to see Dewitt Stamps, who was just emerging from the hotel lobby, bearing the old Bible that he always had with him these days. "Ma'am, I got to take my leave now . . . somebody over there I need to talk to."

Clara Ashworth followed the direction of Luke's gaze. "Him . . . Stamps? That worthless drunkard?"

Luke had already stepped away, but those words stopped him. He turned and glared at the woman. "Mrs. Ashworth, Dewitt Stamps was a drunkard once, but he hasn't been one for a good while now. He ain't had a drink in three years or more that I know of."

"Pshaw!" the woman said. "A drunkard is a drunkard forever."

"Unless he turns away from it," Luke returned. "Dewitt's a man of faith now. As a churchwoman, you ought to be applauding the man and calling him your Christian brother."

The woman looked disgusted. "I've got no use for a drunkard, and whatever kind of religion he may claim, he isn't any 'brother' of mine."

Luke nodded and muttered, "I think I can believe that, Mrs. Ashworth." He went on, glad to leave the self-righteous biddy behind, looking down her nose at his departing form.

"Howdy, Dewitt," Luke called as he neared Dewitt. Dewitt merely grunted softly in reply.

"Why so downcast?" Luke asked. "You feeling all right?"

"Oh, I'm well enough, I reckon. Just discouraged about the durned human race, that's all."

Luke glanced back across the street, watching Mrs. Ashworth walking along haughtily, heading up the street toward her big three-story house. "I know the feeling," he said.

"What brung you over to see me?" Dewitt asked. "When I looked up and seen you coming, it took me back to the old days when you used to arrest me for being drunk. When I seen you coming toward me in those days, it was time to run. But I was always too drunk to do it. You remember that time I ran into a wall trying to get away from you?"

"Yeah, but those days are past now, Dewitt. You're the soberest man in Kansas nowadays."

"Yeah, I am. And I'm proud of it. But I guess pride is its own kind of sin. Do you think it's just as sinful for me to be proud of *not* drinking as it was for me to actually be drinking back in the old days?"

"I don't think so."

"But ain't pride a sin?"

Luke hadn't darkened the door of a church in nearly a decade, and held little by way of theological opinions. But from somewhere a burst of wisdom came and he found an answer for Dewitt.

He glanced back toward the spot where he'd stood while talking to Clara Ashworth. "There's different kinds of pride, I think, one sinful and one not. The kind of pride that involves being better in your own mind than other people, that's the sinful kind."

"What's the other kind?"

"Let me answer you this way. Do you think God is proud of you for not drinking?"

"Well . . . yes. I do."

"Then if you ain't proud of yourself, too, it's kind of like telling God he's wrong. You see? What you think of yourself ought to match up with what the Lord thinks of you, oughtn't it?"

Dewitt frowned, mulling it over. His face brightened. "You're right, Luke. Right as rain! Thank you!"

Luke grinned and winked. "Who knows, Dewitt? I might make a preacher yet."

Dewitt laughed freely at the mental picture of Luke behind a pulpit.

"Hey, I might make a *fine* preacher," Luke said, feigning offense.

Dewitt put away his smile and nodded. "So you might, Luke Cable. I'm sorry for laughing. Who am I to laugh at the notion of God changing folks' lives, after what's happened to me? If you've got the calling, you should heed it."

"Dewitt, truth is I don't feel called to nothing except the breakfast table. I got my pay yesterday. I'd like to invite you to sit down and have breakfast with me over at the Taylor Café. I'll buy. And you can tell me why it is you're feeling down and low about the human race."

"You ain't got to buy me no meal, Luke."

"I know. But I made the offer and would be happy if you'd take it. It'll give me the chance to talk to you a bit."

"Well, I will. You're a good man, Luke Cable."

"I try."

A good meal was something that lifelong impoverished bachelor Dewitt Stamps seldom received, and he ate with such an intense concentration and seriousness that Luke struggled not to grin.

"This is prime, Luke. Prime!"

"Glad you like it, Dewitt. Now tell me what you were mulling over when I come upon you out there."

Dewitt sighed. "Luke, why would anybody want to see somebody like me fall back into the wrong kind of life?"

"What do you mean?"

Dewitt shared the story of Jimmy Wills's attempts to tempt him with whiskey. "Why'd he do that, Luke? Why would he want to see me go wrong?"

"Jimmy's young, and he's a fool. I don't know what else to say. Makes me mad as hell that he'd do that."

"It ain't right. People ought to want good things for other folk."

Luke replied, "Yeah. But a lot don't." He was thinking of Clara Ashworth. "Did you take the drink?"

"I didn't. I stood up against the temptation and he finally went and tossed the whiskey out the door. I won that round. Me and the Lord. But there's a lot of wickedness in this world, and it discourages me," Dewitt said. "It's good that there's folks like you who are willing to fight it."

"I don't know if it's worth it sometimes, Dewitt. I'm not sure I'd have agreed to fill in for Ben Keely if I'd known it would be so hard and he'd be gone so long. I wake up every day wondering who's going to get drunk and hit some other gent, or beat up on his wife, or break something at the saloon. Or who might get shot, or take a shot at me. And all for such a little bit of money that it strains me just to be able to buy a meal or two from time to time. If I'd known, I'd have told Ben Keely to find somebody else to fill in for him while he went traipsing to Kentucky."

"Well, you should have knowed how it would be, having been his deputy before."

"I suppose. But one thing I couldn't have known was how long he'd be gone. Ben was supposed to have been back more than a month ago. But I ain't heard the first word from him, and have no notion what's keeping him from coming back. I agreed to serve as acting marshal for a set time, and that time's well past now. By all rights I should be free to quit, but that would leave the town with no peace officer, and I can't do that."

"You know why I figure he ain't come back? Teke Blevins making them threats against him."

"Nah. Not Ben. He's no coward."

"Teke got out the word that he was going to kill Ben. And Teke is a man to be taken serious."

"The fact remains that Ben wouldn't flee this town just because of threats. I know him too well to believe that." Luke shifted in his chair, restless. "But I wish whatever is keeping him from coming back would go away. I'm ready to leave this marshaling business behind. I'm disappointed in myself,

Dewitt. For a long time I thought I'd be a fine peace officer, but more and more I find myself wishing I was doing anything else but this job. I want to quit. I want to say good-bye to all this, head over to Ellsworth, and ask Sally James to marry me."

"Maybe you ought to do that. The county sheriff. He could take over for you, couldn't he? Whether Ben is back or not? I mean, Wiles is in his county, even if he don't work for the town. The people here are still citizens of Wiles County."

"Yeah, but you know as well as me that he's never paid much attention to the town. Since Wiles has its own law enforcers, he gives his attention to the rest of the county."

"Well, if Wiles quit having its own marshal, maybe he'd have a different way of looking at it." Dewitt stared at the tabletop. "I wish I could help you out somehow, Luke."

"Maybe you can."

Dewitt looked up. "Me? How?"

Luke had his own round of tabletop staring for a moment. He'd brought Dewitt here in order to bring up this very subject, but now that he'd done so he wondered if he'd thought it through sufficiently. Didn't matter. He'd opened the door and now he had to step through.

"Truth is, Dewitt, I need some help in the jail."

"Don't Hank McAdams help you already?"

"Hank only works a few hours a week, and lately his mother's been so sickly he's had to spend most his time taking care of her, and he misses a lot of time. Most times it don't make much difference. This is a calm town, typically, and usually one man is enough to handle what comes up. But sometimes I get into a bad situation when I've got somebody locked up at the jail. You can't just leave prisoners by theirselves, not for long, anyway. But when I'm down in the jail office nursemaiding some old drunk, I can't be out in town looking out for the town."

"You need a jailer," said Dewitt. "Somebody to watch the jail so you and Hank can be out taking care of the people."

"Exactly," Luke replied. "So what do you say, Dewitt? You want the job?"

Dewitt's eyes widened. "Me?"

"You see anybody else at this table I could be asking?"

"But, Luke, I . . . I got a job."

"Washing down horses at Baxter's Livery ain't the best of jobs, my friend."

"No . . . but it's one I've done for a long time now. And Mr. Baxter's been good to me. Lets me live in that room in the livery loft."

"That loft is a shabby place, Dewitt. And Mr. Baxter's been good to you because he figures the town drunk is the only person who'd be willing to work that job for what little it pays. And it's a job you could do about as well drunk as sober, so you were a good fit."

"That's all past now, Luke. I don't get drunk no more."

"No. But you're still living in a shack like you did before, and I doubt Baxter's paying you any more than he did before just because you've gone sober. I'm offering you something better. A little more pay, and you can live in that little house out behind the jail. That's part of the jail property, you know. It's not much, but it's better than that drafty livery room, and you'll be doing work that's got some dignity to it. You'll work for the city, just like I do. You'll have a title: Deputy Jailer."

All this seemed more than Dewitt could absorb. He looked at Luke as if the man had just sprouted wings and begun speaking the language of angels. "Luke, you really got the power to do that? I mean, right now you're the acting marshal, but that ain't the same as being the *real* marshal, like Ben Keely. What if the town won't let you hire me? What if they say I'm just a sorry old drunk not fit for the job?"

"Then I'd say back to them that you're not a drunk anymore, that even when you were a drunk you still did good work at the livery and proved yourself reliable, and that if they won't give me the help I need to do my own job, they can find themselves somebody else to fill in for Ben Keely."

"You'd do that?"

"I would."

"Bless your heart, Luke Cable! You're a blessing of God to this old sinner."

"Dewitt, that might be the finest compliment I've ever been given. You want that coffee warmed up? Mine's getting a little cold."

He lifted a hand and signaled for the waiter. Dewitt just sat grinning at him, eyes moist with tears of gratitude.

It was then that Luke began to worry. What if Dewitt had a point about the town leaders? What if they declined his bid to hire a deputy jailer? Especially one with as unpolished a past as Dewitt Stamps's?

If they balked, would Luke really walk away from his job?

He watched as the waiter refilled his cup, then turned his eyes to the window and stared across the street beyond.

Come back, Ben, he mentally pleaded. *Come back and start doing your job again, so I can quit doing it for you.*

CHAPTER THREE

That evening, Luke Cable strode along the Jones Street boardwalk with Henry Myers, mayor of Wiles. He'd encountered Myers randomly, and the chance meeting had given him the opportunity he needed to discuss the prospects he'd discussed over breakfast with Dewitt Stamps.

"Dewitt, huh?" Myers said. "Well, that's not a name I'd have expected to hear put forth for a position in law enforcement. Not two or three years ago, anyway."

"I know exactly what you mean. Dewitt used to be no end of trouble to Ben and me. Had to lock him up two, three times a week sometimes. But the man seems to have honest-to-God reformed himself."

"Do you truly believe he can be trusted to oversee the jailing of men he used to drink with? Because there'll be some of those. They might be able to talk him into being lax with them."

Luke shook his head. "I don't think so. Not anymore. Most of those who Dewitt used to drink with avoid him now. He's quick to preach at them, you see. Try to push religion on them. They don't much like that. Having Dewitt oversee the jail is likely to make the jail a place they strongly want to avoid.

Can you imagine being an old drunk, locked up in a cage with Dewitt Stamps looking through the bars with that glaring eye of his, telling you how you need to get on the straight and narrow?"

The mayor pondered the image, grinned, then laughed. "A good point, Luke. Ha!"

"So I can hire him?"

"At the pay rate we discussed, yes. Keeping in mind that Ben Keely might not wish to perpetuate that hire when he returns. The town would have to take his views into account. Assuming, that is, that Ben would be allowed to continue as marshal."

"What are you getting at?"

"Luke, when Ben left, it was under a clear and written understanding that he would be gone for only a limited time, then would return to full duties. He has violated that agreement and has not even made contact by letter or wire to explain his circumstances or his intentions. Though I think the world of Ben and am inclined to give him the benefit of the doubt, most on the town council are past their limit of patience. They are pleased with the job you've been doing in Ben's stead, and I think Ben, when he returns, will find himself hard-pressed to find favor on the council for the idea of him continuing as town marshal. Unless he can provide a compelling explanation for his negligence."

"So does this mean I might be in line to have this marshaling job permanent?"

"A likely possibility. If you'll have it."

"I'd have to give it thought. It's a task that drains a man of his energy and spirit. And the pay ain't good. Even with me drawing the full marshal's pay during Ben's absence, it's been nothing to put much into my pocket. Not that I ain't grateful for the opportunity. Don't take me wrong on that."

Myers had grown serious. "Luke, let me ask you something, since we're in a private setting here. I hate even raising this kind of question, but I must: do you believe that Ben Keely is still alive?"

Luke stopped walking and faced the mayor. Both men glanced about to ensure that they were out of earshot of anyone else on the street. "The thought has crossed my mind that something could have happened to Ben," Luke said. "It just ain't in Ben's character to neglect his duties and just run off, without a word. And besides, I know for a fact he wasn't inclined to stay back home in Kentucky. It was hard for him even to get up the will to go back at all, even with his father dying and all. Problems in his family, you see. He's got a sister he's estranged from, and with his parents both dead and gone, she's all that's left for him back home, and I doubt he'd stay because of her. If you'd asked me, I'd have predicted he'd come back sooner than planned, not later."

"The question now is whether he will come back at all. I was aware of this sister you talk about. In fact, when Ben failed to return on schedule, I wired the rail station in his Kentucky town, trying to get a message to Ben, if he's still there, or his sister. Bess, I think her name is."

"What was the reply?" asked Luke.

"No reply at all from Ben or his sister either one. The only reply I got came from the key operator himself. He knew the family. You know how it is in small places like that. Anyhow, he told me that Ben had been there, sure enough, but wasn't there any longer. He'd headed back here to Kansas, apparently."

"If he did, he never got here. Or never showed himself here, anyway. I have to wonder if that key operator knew what he was talking about."

"I have the same question. And along with it, a bad feeling I can't shake off. Something just feels wrong, you know. Ben just isn't the kind to vanish and not let anybody know what's going on. As loco as it sounds to say it out loud, I've caught myself wondering if that sister of his maybe has done him in."

"Were things that bad with the two of them?"

Myers sighed. "I think maybe so. As good friends as me and Ben have been, he never talked to me about her much. The subject always seemed to trouble him whenever it came up. He told me she was strange. That was his word for her. 'Strange.' Said she shamed the family and her parents and hurt her own reputation by her ways."

"Wayward woman?"

"He never said it outright. But I suppose yes. That was the only interpretation I could attach to his words, anyway."

"Even then, though, that wouldn't mean she'd be the kind to kill her own brother. Hell, we don't even know he's dead, so we don't know that *anybody* killed him."

"But we do know he ain't come back to his work, and that ain't like Ben Keely." The mayor shook his head and rubbed a hand across his chin. "Something's wrong somewhere, Luke. Don't you feel it?"

Luke slumped and sighed. "I do. I do."

They didn't talk much after that. When they parted, Luke turned before he walked away and said, "Thank you again, Mayor, for letting me hire Dewitt as a jailer."

"I hope his presence makes your job a little easier. Has it?"

"It will. No question about it."

They went their separate ways, both of them musing through dark wonderings about what might have happened to Ben Keely.

The next day Luke, not content with secondhand information from the mayor, went to the nearest telegraph office and had a wire sent to Ben Keely's hometown in Kentucky, to be delivered to Bess Keely, asking for any information she might provide about her brother's whereabouts.

The message he received in reply came back from the key operator on the other end, just as the mayor's had done. It told Luke that Ben Keely had been in Kentucky but now was absent. The general belief was that he had traveled back to Kansas as had been his plan, but the railroad's records showed nothing to indicate Keely had left by train. His arrival was on record and a return ticket had been purchased, too, along with space in a stable car to ship home the horse he'd brought with him, but the return ticket had not been used, nor the horse ever actually stabled and shipped.

This information merely confirmed for Luke what the mayor had already told him, but there was one additional piece of news. His telegram could not be sent to Bess Keely as Luke had requested. Bess Keely had vanished as well, and no one knew where she might have gone, or why.

No comfort in that information, certainly. If the sister had fled, she was doing so for a reason. Something to hide or something to hide from. Or perhaps she'd suffered the same lethal fate as her brother, if Ben in fact was dead.

Either way, Luke couldn't shake the feeling that he wasn't going to see Ben Keely again. Ben's marshaling days, probably his *living* days, were over. It was merely a suspicion, but one that shouted in Luke's mind in a volume approaching that of full knowledge.

Luke walked the streets of his town, crumpled transcript of the key operator's message in his hand. Cursing softly, he tossed it into the space below the nearest board sidewalk.

Time to go back to the jailhouse. There was a prisoner to see to. Young fellow who'd gotten into a fight and took it too far, leaving the other fighter with a cut that required stitching up by old Doc Murray.

Then Luke remembered: Dewitt was at the jail tonight. He *had* help. So he didn't have to go back to his office after all.

Not that he could go home. He still had rounds to make. Town laws to enforce. Lord, it wore a man out sometimes.

Luke spoke softly to no one present. "Ben, maybe

you ain't dead. Maybe you just decided to throw it all away and just not come back. If so, I'm mad at you for it. But I understand why you done it. Lord knows I understand."

He turned on his heel and headed back into the heart of town.

CHAPTER FOUR

Two days later, a broadly built, tall man with a mustache that hung half an inch over his lip and crawled over both sides of his leathery face rode into Wiles on a huge roan horse. On the man's vest was a badge, tarnished so that it blended in with the vest's leather and was hardly visible past ten feet away.

He turned down an alleyway and crossed over to Montague Street. There he paused, slumping in the saddle, and admired the most remarkable edifice in the little Kansas town: a three-story, gleaming white structure with a front porch worthy of a state capitol building. The man tipped back his hat and studied the building from bottom to top, noting the way the letters on the sign identifying the building stood out brightly in the sunlight.

The sign read:

MONTAGUE'S EMPORIUM
Fine Clothing, Dry Goods
Hardware, Notions, and Domestic Products for
All Purposes
Founder and Proprietor: Campbell Montague

A figure strode from the boardwalk fronting the building and neared the man on horseback. "Good evening, Sheriff Crowe," said the newcomer, Clara Ashworth.

Her voice startled him. He looked down at her sharply, his hand actually moving spasmodically in the direction of the Remington holstered high on his right hip. But he caught himself, relaxed, and smiled down on her.

"Good day, ma'am. Mrs. Ashworth, if I remember correctly? Wife of Howard Ashworth from down at the bank?"

"Indeed, Sheriff," she said, extending up her hand to let him gently shake it. "It is a pleasure to see the leading peace officer of our county making a visit to town. Nothing is amiss, I hope?"

"Just here on business, ma'am. Hoping to locate your town marshal to help me conduct it."

She rolled her eyes to the clouds above. "Oh my, sir, don't get me to talking on *that* subject! Our town marshal is someone you will not find. Marshal Keely has not graced our town with his presence for lo these many weeks now. We've been making do for law enforcement with our young deputy, Mr. Cable, while awaiting Marshal Keely's overdue return."

"Yes, ma'am. I'm aware that Ben went away eastward to visit his kin owing to the death of his father. It's Mr. Cable I've come to find."

"Perhaps he is at his office, then."

"I'm on my way over there. Just crossed over through the alley there to take a look at the emporium here. Remarkable that such a place exists in a town such as Wiles."

Mrs. Ashworth frowned. " 'A town such as Wiles.' What is the meaning of that phrase, sir? It seemed to have an overtone of insult . . . and given that I am a descendant of James Wiles, whose name this county and town bears, I cannot let such a comment pass without asking for clarification."

Sheriff Harvey Crowe inwardly cursed at himself for having forgotten the uppity nature of this woman. He deplored having to pander to her prideful manner, but the fact was that her husband had been a strong supporter of his first bid for county sheriff years ago, and he felt a certain obligation.

"Ma'am, I was merely talking about the fine nature of the store in relation to the size of the town. No reference intended to any perceived deficiency in your town's quality." *Like hell*, he mentally added. Crowe had never liked this town, largely because of the social pretentiousness of some of its residents, foremost among them Mrs. Clara Ashworth.

"I accept your apology, then," she said, although he'd apologized for nothing.

He held his tongue.

Clara inflated with pompousness. "In my own view, the fact that Mr. Montague chose our town for his notable establishment is indicative that he is insightful enough to recognize quality and potential when he sees it. He could have built his emporium anywhere he pleased. Wichita. Denver. Chicago. But he chose Wiles, Kansas."

"Yes, ma'am. I've talked to him about that. He told me that he wanted to find a place where he could live out his later years peaceful and all, and where that idiot nephew of his wouldn't be picked on as much as he would be in a big city."

A look of disgust passed across the woman's face. "Oh, yes . . . that nephew . . . the only negative aspect I can find regarding this institution's presence in our town. It's a public embarrassment to have that drooling fool out here sweeping these steps and singing in that horrible voice of his, day after day. I'm quite sure it turns away customers and drives people away from one of the commercial areas of our town, yet Mr. Montague allows it to go on."

"I don't think Mr. Montague cares as much about drawing customers as he does about having something to occupy his time and give his nephew something to do," Crowe answered.

"Well, if that is so, then I am surprised at the success he has had in life. As Howard always says, a man of business must be unaffected by sentiment. Opening such a massive business as a pastime and working opportunity for an idiot boy . . . that is hardly sound business reasoning."

Crowe touched the front brim of his hat. "I have to move on, ma'am. Have yourself a pleasant—" He cut off abruptly, having glanced up at the upper front portion of the emporium building, where a window overlooked the street.

"What do you see, Sheriff?" Mrs. Ashworth asked.

"I . . . I'm not sure, ma'am," he said. "Trick of the light on the window glass, probably. As I was saying, have a pleasant day."

He took his leave of Clara Ashworth, glad to do so. When he was away from her, the woman looked up at the high window of the emporium, squinted, shrugged, and moved on.

Dewitt Stamps was dozing at the jailer's desk when his unexpected visitor showed up at his office door. He came awake at the sound of the knock, stood so fast he bumped over his chair, and brushed down his rumpled hair and clothing as he called, "Hang on! Be right there!"

He was not pleased to see County Sheriff Harvey Crowe on the other side of the door. More than once he'd had encounters with the hard-edged lawman during his drinking days, and he didn't anticipate that Crowe would be the kind to believe he'd really changed.

Crowe immediately fulfilled Dewitt's expectation. "Well, Stamps, I see the tales are really true," he said, flinty eyes boring into the disheveled jailer. Crowe scanned Dewitt up and down. "They've hired an egg-sucking dog to guard the henhouse. Hell, you look like you just woke up, man. Does the acting marshal know you've been snoozing on the job?"

"I'm wide awake, Sheriff. You want to come in?"

Crowe grunted and entered, giving Dewitt a sniff as he did so. "Well, you don't smell like whiskey, anyway, so that's good."

"I've give up the stuff," Dewitt said proudly. "The good Lord runs my life now."

"Yeah, I heard somewhere you'd gone religious on us, Stamps," Crowe replied. "Good for you, then. Hope it sticks."

"Four years now," Dewitt said.

Crowe gave a dismissive shake of the head. "For most I've known, being a drunk is a lifetime matter. You got plenty of time and opportunity to fall off that wagon, Dewitt."

"I won't. I'm riding that wagon from here on out. Lord's wagon."

"We'll see. I hope you're right. But even the Lord's wagon hits bumps that can jar a man off his seat sometimes. Hey, where's the town marshal?"

"Ben's been gone off to Kentucky now for a good while," Dewitt said. "I thought you knew that."

"I *do* know that," Crowe returned with irritation. "I'm asking for Luke, not Ben. Acting Marshal Cable."

"Well, I ain't sure where Luke is just now," said Dewitt. "Probably out making some rounds. He does that most of the time if he ain't here in the office."

"Well, I guess I'm going to have to track him down, then," Crowe growled. "If he comes back in here in the next little while, you tell him I'm looking for him. If I don't find him I'll check back here and see if he's come back."

"I'll do it, Sheriff. Is there something wrong?"

"Mostly just something strange. I got a wire this morning from over near the Doggett community. You know Charlie Bays, who's got that little ranch out that way? Well, one of Charlie's boys, the one with the big knot on the side of his head that looks like a brown egg growing hair, has found a leg out by the railroad track."

Dewitt paled. "A leg? Like a cut-off leg?"

"Exactly. Leg, still in a trouser leg, boot still on the foot. Lying there beside the tracks."

"Oh my," muttered Dewitt, slumping weakly back toward his chair at the desk. "Oh *my!*"

"You look a little green, Stamps. This kind of thing make you squeamish?"

"It's just that . . . that . . . you know what I'm thinking about."

"Yep. You're thinking back on all the times you passed out drunk by the railroad tracks, and how some of them times you probably had a leg or an arm lying over the rail, and how but for the grace of God and good luck you never were lying there like that when the train actually came along. You're thinking how easy it could have been your leg somebody was finding by the railroad."

Dewitt nodded weakly, staring at the top of the desk.

"That's what it'll prove to be, you know," Crowe said. "Some old drunk's leg. Some poor guzzling bastard who had the ill fortune to pass out while he was walking the tracks and drinking. What is it about you drunks that makes you walk on railroad tracks, anyhow? It's always that way with you people . . . moth to the flame. Moth to the flame. Every drunk I've ever known ends up passed out along a railroad track sometime or another, when he could just as easy have walked up a road or a footpath instead of a railroad track." Crowe paused, cleared his throat, and began speaking in a mocking, higher-pitched voice. "Oh, I'm so drunk I'm going to fall over and pass out any second now . . . I think I'll run down and straddle the railroad tracks." Then Crowe laughed derisively.

Dewitt had nothing to say.

Crowe found a chair in the corner and dragged it over near the desk. Dewitt did a poor job of disguising his displeasure at this. Crowe was not pleasant company to have close at hand. Too many memories of past arrests.

"I wonder if Wilton Brand is in town?" Crowe said. "If he is, it might be worth taking him along, too, him being coroner."

"Why you need a coroner for just a leg? A leg ain't a dead man."

"No. But Wilton knows how to read the flesh, so to speak. He can probably tell me how long ago that leg got cut off, how big a man it belonged to, all that kind of thing."

"He's probably over at his shop."

"I'll find him. Meantime, you keep an eye out for Luke. I want to take him with me, too."

"Why you want Luke? He ain't got no authority over in Doggett. He's just the marshal here in Wiles."

"He's also deputized to work with me in the county, just like I help him out here in town. Cooperation, Dewitt. Helps us both. And besides, I have a funny feeling about this whole thing. Charlie Bays says that he don't believe that leg was cut off by a train, even though it was lying beside the tracks and the first thing you think of in that kind of situation is that it had to be a train accident."

"Why's Charlie think otherwise?"

"Something about the way it looks, I guess. That's why I want the coroner with me. He ought to be able to render a good judgment."

Dewitt said, "I'm glad I ain't no coroner. I ain't good with dead things and blood and such."

"Nobody's 'good with' that kind of thing, Dewitt. But when something's your job, you learn to deal with it. So you want to come along, too?"

Dewitt shook his head firmly. "No, sir. I was told by Luke to mind the jail office and keep an eye on our prisoner. That's what I'm going to do. My job here is deputy jailer, not deputy cut-off-leg looker."

"Who you got back there? Anybody I know?"

"Stu Curtis."

"Drunk as usual?"

"Yes, sir."

"Hopeless case."

"No, sir. Ain't no hopeless cases. I'm proof of that."

"Time will tell. Though I'll admit to you, Dewitt, that four years off the bottle is right impressive, given how you used to be."

"Power of the Lord, Sheriff. That's all it is."

Crowe wasn't listening. He'd just spotted someone across the street, and headed out the door without another word to Dewitt.

The person he'd spotted was the local physician, Dr. Bill Artemus, who had retired from medicine in Boston, headed west to settle into a private, relaxed life in a small Kansas town, and there had found himself busier than he'd been in the city. Sheriff Crowe called him down, crossed the street to him, and talked to him animatedly while Dewitt Stamps, standing by his desk, watched it all through the jail office window. When Crowe walked off, the aged but nimble doctor went with him. They headed toward Cross Street, where Coroner Wilton Brand maintained his furniture shop at the times he wasn't dealing with the dead of Wiles County.

"Going to go see that leg, the whole gang of them, I guess," Dewitt muttered aloud to himself. Then he shuddered, hoping he'd never have to go look at such a gruesome thing in the course of his humble law enforcement duties.

Dewitt was about to sit down again when he noticed Crowe grinning and waving at someone down the street. Dewitt shifted his angle of view and saw that the person Crowe had seen was Luke Cable.

"Going to have a regular parade to go out to Charlie Bays's ranch," Dewitt said to himself, then sat down.

CHAPTER FIVE

The severed leg had been moved into Charlie Bays's shed by the time the delegation from Wiles got to the Bays Ranch at Doggett. Because of his hounds, Charlie Bays explained. Had to move it for fear of the dogs treating it like found food. Funny thing, though, he added: the dogs that had sniffed the leg out in the first place had not seemed nearly as interested in it as canines normally would be.

"Maybe they just weren't hungry," Luke speculated with a shrug as he followed Sheriff Crowe toward the shed. At the door he paused and took a deep breath, expecting that the smell of the leg might be hard to tolerate, depending on how long it had been severed.

The air in the shed, though, smelled only slightly musty. No smell of decay at all. Evidence, Luke figured, that the leg had not been long separated from its former possessor.

When he saw the limb, however, he rethought that notion. The leg was lying on a rugged shed table, bare, Bays having slipped off the trouser leg that had apparently been cut off with it.

The boot, worn and dirty, was still on the foot. The flesh of the leg was quite pale, somewhat hirsute but lacking freckles, blemishes, and the like. The violence of dismemberment had not marred the leg in any very noticeable way.

Coroner Wilton Brand moved to the severed, thigh portion of the leg, leaned over, and examined the cut flesh closely. He waved Dr. Artemus over. "Take a look, Bill. You see what I see?"

The aging physician joined the coroner. Both men looked intently at the leg. Artemus spoke first. "I'll be! I do see it!"

"What is it?" Crowe asked.

"This leg was not cut off by a train wheel," the doctor said.

Brand jumped in. "And beyond that, it was not severed from the body of a living man."

"What?" Crowe moved around to join Brand and Artemus at the wound end of the severed limb.

"Wilton, you're right," Dr. Artemus said. "I'd not even noticed that." He probed the exposed, cut muscle with his finger, causing Crowe to shudder and pull back reflexively. "Very strange," Artemus said. "Almost like . . . I don't know . . . leather. Or jerked meat. This is embalming beyond any degree I've ever encountered before. This leg is essentially . . . mummified."

Wilton Brand nodded. "The very word that came to my mind, too. That might explain the lack of great interest on the part of the dogs. The flesh has been altered enough to have a scent that puts them off rather than appeals to them."

Crowe spoke. "Before we wander too far afield, gentlemen, let's get back to the first thing you said.

How do you know this was not cut off beneath a train, especially considering that the leg was found beside the tracks?"

"Two reasons, the first being that this leg has been heavily embalmed, and in a manner quite uncommon. Second, there's the nature of the cut. The edges of the sever wound are sharp and precise," said the doctor. "And I see no evidence of the kind of massive pinching and crushing that would have been caused by train wheels. It appears to me that this leg was removed in a much more surgical fashion. And look . . . see the bone? See how cleanly and neatly it is cut? And there are marks visible on it that appear consistent with those left by a surgical bone saw."

Crowe frowned. "So somebody cut the leg off a mummified dead man, cut his trouser leg off, too, and slid the leg back into it, boot and all, and laid it beside a railroad track on a Kansas flatland so it would look like it had been cut off by a train at the same time. Is that what you're telling me?"

"Odd as it may seem, that is the evidence that my eye sees."

"And mine," said Brand.

Crowe turned to Charlie Bays. "Nobody actually saw the accident or whatever it was that resulted in this leg being where it was, right, Charlie? Nobody ever saw somebody actually getting his leg pinched off under a train wheel?"

"That's right."

"But you still think it was cut off by a passing train."

"I did . . . but now these men have raised my doubts," the rancher replied. "It just don't look . . . well, messed up enough to have been cut off by train wheels."

"It's the mummification that mystifies me," said Brand. "I'm no undertaker, just a coroner, but I think I can tell you authoritatively that dead flesh is not commonly preserved in this kind of state. The leathery condition of the internal flesh . . . I can't account for it. This leg was preserved by uncommon, highly expert means."

Crowe shook his head and spoke to Luke. "See why I wanted you here, Luke? This whole situation is so damn strange that I wanted somebody else along to understand it, too."

Luke scuffed his foot in the dirt. " 'Understand' isn't the right word in this case," he said. "This just has me perplexed."

"What do you want me to do with this leg?" asked Bays. "My Franny is all worked up about it being out here in our shed. She wants it gone, and truth is so do I."

Luke turned to Wilton Brand. "Wilton, it ain't a corpse, but it's part of one. Could you as coroner take charge of it for now? Keep it stored? If it's mummified, it ought not to decay on you, at least not very fast."

"I'll put it in the morgue," he said, referring to what was in fact little more than a small barn with a tightly enclosed room he used as a coroner's facility and short-term morgue. It stood on the edge of town, near his home and on his property, and he leased it to the county for a dollar a year. "I want to study it, anyway, to see if I can figure out some of how that thing got into that preserved state. I'll bring in Mr. Edgar from the undertaking parlor and see what he has to say."

"Thank you, Wilton," Crowe said. "I suspect that leg may prove to be evidence in a crime."

"I know what you're thinking," Luke said. "You're thinking that whoever cut off that leg and put it out where it was found was trying to make it appear that it had been cut off by a passing train. Which means they were trying to disguise what really happened."

"Right. If the intention wasn't deception, why include the trouser leg? Why leave the boot on the foot? The goal was to make what had happened seem obvious. But in this case, the 'obvious' isn't actually obvious, if you take the time to look closely."

"Now, I guess, all we need to do is find a mummified dead man hopping around town because he's missing his left leg," Luke said, grinning.

"Wilton, fetch up that leg," Crowe said. "Charlie, we'll take our leave of you now. And you can tell Franny she won't have to hesitate to come out to her shed anymore."

The battered coffeepot steaming on the stove in Luke Cable's office filled the entire jail with a strong but delicious coffee aroma. Luke, Dewitt, Harvey Crowe, and Wilton Brand sat lazily about the room, cups in hand, talking over what had just gone on.

Dewitt, having not been part of the group that traveled to the ranch, was full of questions.

"So how can they be so sure it wasn't a train that cut the leg off?" he asked for the third time.

Crowe rolled his eyes in exasperation, so Luke fielded the question this time. "It's because of how it was cut," he said. "Think about it, Dewitt . . . even though it's not pleasant thinking. If a train cuts off a man's leg, that's going to mash the wound area right considerable, and crush through the bone. Not very neat work. But this leg was sliced as neat and clean as if some surgeon had worked on it. And the bone looked sawed. Not crushed, but sawed."

"Another thing, too," Brand added. "And I didn't think about this until we were riding back. That leg was severed about as high up as you could cut off a leg. Nigh up to the hip, and straight across. I can't figure how a man could lie on a railroad track and get his leg cut off at that particular angle without losing more of himself than just that one leg. Not if he'd just chanced to pass out and fall down. You'd pretty much have to lie crossways on the track to lose your leg at that straight of an angle, and if you were doing that, the other leg would be cut off, too. But they only found the one leg. That alone to me is evidence that somebody placed that leg there after it had already been surgically removed from a corpse. A corpse, by the way, that had been embalmed in some manner unknown to the science of undertaking."

"Strangest thing I've ever run across," Crowe said.

"I wonder if that leg was throwed off the train by somebody riding on it," Dewitt said.

Crowe rolled his eyes again. It was his habit to perceive and treat anything said by Dewitt Stamps as derision-worthy. "Riding the train, or the leg?" he said, then laughed heartily.

"Sheriff, come on now," Luke said, reflexively slipping into a defensive attitude toward Dewitt.

"Well, it was just how he phrased it," the sheriff replied.

"We all know what he meant, and I think Dewitt has a point," Luke said. "This is a small community. Somebody loses a limb around here, people would know. And I doubt there's a lot of mummified corpses lying around, either. I'd say odds are high that somebody passing through on the train disposed of that leg, figuring everybody would think exactly what we first thought . . . that somebody lost the leg underneath the train."

"Makes a man wonder what's going on, what the real story is," Crowe said. He sipped his coffee. "Hell, this town is full of mysteries, if you look close enough. Like who the devil was it I saw looking out of that upper window of the emporium earlier today? I was out in the street talking to old Mrs. Self-righteous Ashworth. I looked up at that high window on the front of the emporium, and there was somebody looking out. I thought it was old Montague at first, for it was a man's face and looked like his, but this fellow had a full white beard, and Montague is clean-shaved."

"It probably *was* Montague," Luke said. "The

'beard' part was probably just light shining on the glass."

"I don't think so," said Crowe. "I'm putting a few years behind me, no question of that, but my eyes are still strong."

"Anybody can be fooled by shadows and reflections," Luke said. "I'm not aware of anybody living at the emporium except for Montague himself and his nephew Macky. You know any different than that, Dewitt?"

Crowe spoke first. "Hell, as much as Dewitt has drunk over the years, he's probably seen Jesus Christ and Moses working down at the saddle shop while the prophet Isaiah pees in the outhouse out back."

Dewitt ignored the jibe and answered Luke. "I ain't aware of anybody but them two living at the emporium, either. Mr. Montague's got his big house in behind the emporium, and Macky's room is off to the side. But nobody lives in that upper part. Up where that window is, there's nothing but a big old storage attic. I know. I was up there once, carrying something up for Mr. Montague."

"My eyes are good. I seen what I seen," Crowe said.

"Good Lord, I know what *I'm* seeing right now!" said Wilton Brand. He was half raised out of his chair, propping himself so he had a better view out the window. "Look at that, gents! You *ever* seen a woman hauling around such a pair?"

Every man in the room, save Dewitt, was at the window in a moment. Dewitt closed his eyes and seemed to be praying silently. He knew who they were looking at. Had to be the same woman, Katrina whoever-she-was, who'd come down the stairs at the hotel that morning he'd had the conversation with Jimmy Wills over in the Gable House. Wanting to avoid the sin of lust, Dewitt knew better than to let himself look out that window.

The other men clearly had no similar scruples. They stared and commented lewdly and stayed so fixed on what they were watching that Dewitt could tell the moment the woman went out of sight. They all moved as one back to their chairs, shaking their heads as if they'd just witnessed an awesome marvel of nature.

Wilton Brand, known by all as a lecherous soul, could hardly keep from stirring out of his seat. He grinned at Crowe. "Tell you what, Sheriff, if I was a lawman, I'd find cause to investigate that there woman! Just for the chance to look at her!"

"I never knew you to need a pretext for looking at a woman, Wilton," Crowe replied.

"You're right about that, my friend!" declared Brand.

"Well, the law might *have* good reason to look into what that woman's doing," said Dewitt.

"How so?" asked Luke.

Dewitt hesitated. "I hate to talk about such things, not knowing for sure. A man's accusations ought to be firm, you know."

Crowe sighed loudly. "Ah, hell, Dewitt, quit fretting over every little thing and say what you got to say."

Dewitt nodded. "All right, then. A while back I was over in the lobby of the Gable House, morning hours, just reading my Bible. Jimmy Wills had been up night clerking and said that all through the night, there was men coming in and going up to see that woman. Katrina . . . Katrina . . ."

"Haus, I think," Luke said.

"Yeah. Anyway, Jimmy had it figured she was selling herself up in her room, you know."

"Well, if she is, she's got a good product for drawing customers," said Wilton Brand. "Lord, I might find myself paying a visit to her myself, if I can do it without Lawman Luke here catching me!"

Luke tried to keep the conversation more maturely focused. "Is she really whoring herself, Dewitt?"

"That's what Jimmy said. That's all I know. I never saw none of it happening myself. Just saw her come down the stairs and go out onto the street, that's all."

"Well, all joking aside here, if she's using the hotel for the practice of prostitution, I intend to see that brought to an end. Ain't going to happen in *my* town!"

Crowe snorted with laughter. "Luke, boy, who do you think you're fooling here? There's always been soiled doves in Wiles County, and in Wiles itself. I've locked a few of them up from time to time, but the fact is there ain't much gain in trying to halt that kind of thing. It's been around as long as there's been people, and it ain't likely to go away."

"Not without the power of God," threw in Dewitt, to Crowe's obvious annoyance.

"Well, I can't sit back and let it go if I've been told about it," Luke responded. "That would be negligence of my duty."

"Do what you got to do, then," Crowe said. "I, for one, am an officer of the law who prefers to spend his time fighting crimes that actually hurt people."

Luke shrugged.

"Would I be gossiping if I told you something I seen that might have something to do with this?" Dewitt said.

"If it's something we need to know to enforce the law, I think you ought to tell," Luke replied.

"Well . . . all right. It was two nights ago. I was out walking in town because I'd finished up my work here and there was nobody to watch in the jail. I figured a little exercise might make me sleep better, so I walked. Kept an eye on things while I did, kind of like making rounds like you do, Luke."

"I appreciate that, Dewitt."

"Anyway, I was over near the Gable House and thought about stopping in to say hello to Jimmy Wills, figuring he was working the night duty as usual. But I never actual went into the hotel lobby. I stopped in the alley for a piss there across the street from the hotel, and when I was coming out to cross the street, I seen somebody I recognized going into the hotel. And I wondered why he'd be out visiting the hotel at that hour of the night. So I kind of watched, and through them front windows that look into the staircase over near where it goes down into the lobby, I could see him going up. And I remembered that woman living there, and it come to me what he was up to. Surprised me, I got to say."

"Who was it, Dewitt?" asked Crowe.

Dewitt opened his mouth and closed it again, frowning. "Go on and tell, Dewitt," Luke said.

"Howard Ashworth," Dewitt said softly.

There was silence as the group took it in. Then Crowe chuckled softly, the chuckle growing into a full laugh that spread to the others. Luke managed not to join the laughter, but couldn't suppress a smile.

"Oooh, Lordy!" Crowe said. "Can't say I can hold old Ashworth much at fault for that sin, considering what he's got to go home to!"

"Typical old hypocrite!" said Wilton Brand in a tone almost triumphant. "Just the kind of thing you can expect from them what wave their religion like a banner over everybody else they think they're better than! Old church elder Ashworth sits there on that pew with his old cow of a wife Sunday after Sunday, singing praises to heaven, and all the while he's sneaking out in the night making his own kind of heaven with a whore in the hotel! Bah! That's what keeps me out of church. All the damned hypocrites!"

"Why, Wilton, even if you ain't a churchgoer, I thought you professed to be a man of faith," Luke said. "Ain't that so?"

"I got faith. I just ain't one to go strut it down the street every Sunday morning to put on a show of going to church."

"So you got faith. To that extent, then, you're the same as Ashworth."

"Yeah, to that extent."

"But just now you were looking out that window at that woman and talking about how you might go dally with a fallen woman. So you're like Ashworth to that extent, too."

"What are you saying, Luke?"

Luke shrugged and winked at Dewitt on the

sneak. "Just saying, Wilton, that apparently you don't have to go to church to be a hypocrite."

"Hell, I ain't no hypocrite! I don't go waltzing down to the Presbyterian church every Sunday and put on a righteous show so everybody can see what a 'fine Christian' I am like Ashworth does!"

"No, but you said just now you were a man of faith. And that right after talking about your plan, or at least your wish, to go sin with a whore. Sinning with a whore is against the law of the Lord, Wilton, last time I checked. So that makes you as big a hypocrite as Ashworth, whether or not you sit on the pew at the Presbyterian church. That's the gospel according to Luke Cable, anyway."

"Amen!" Dewitt Stamps bellowed out. "You preach it, Luke!"

Brand nearly came out of his chair. He aimed a finger at Dewitt. "I'll hear no more from the likes of *you*, you old drunk!" Then he looked at Luke. "As for you, Marshal Cable, I never thought I'd hear such an insult from somebody I took to be a friend."

"Why, we *are* friends, Wilton. And friends can talk honest with each other. That's all I was doing, just talking honest."

"Calling me a hypocrite, that's what you were doing!"

"Same as you were doing about Ashworth."

"But I *ain't* a hypocrite, and he is!"

"Whatever you say, Wilton, even though I think I've made a strong case otherwise."

"Hell, Luke Cable, I'm as damn fine a Christian man as you'll run across! I ain't got a hypocrite's bone in my whole damn body! Hell *fire*, man!"

"Glory hallelujah to you, too, Wilton."

Brand swore again, came to his feet, and stomped out of the office, slamming the door as he went.

Crowe laughed. "You got his goat that time, Luke! Got his goat, roasted it whole, and ate it with taters! Ha!"

CHAPTER SIX

Two days later, Luke had cause to think back on the conversation in the jail office when he was walking along Emporium Street and two things simultaneously caught his eye. One was a flyer freshly tacked to the wall of the empty dress shop at the intersection of Emporium Street and Smith Alley, across the street from the emporium. The other was the attention-grabbing form of Katrina Haus flouncing and bouncing across the street, stack of papers in her hand, toward the big staircase of the emporium. On that staircase, sweeping with his usual seriousness and intensity, was Macky Montague, the mentally underdeveloped nephew of the emporium's founder and operator, Campbell Montague.

Macky took no seeming notice of the woman until she was halfway up the staircase; then she caught his eye and he froze, gripping his broom so tightly it looked as if he might break it. Macky's eyes kept drifting from the woman's face to her chest and back again. Luke had to grin. Macky might be mentally limited, but he was a man all the same, and a vision such as Katrina Haus could not fail to catch even his innocent eye.

Katrina noticed Macky and turned toward him,

studying him closely. Luke could not tell whether she was enjoying his obvious discomfort or simply found him interesting for some reason. "Good morning, young man," she said in a clear, delicate voice made musical by the hint of a foreign accent Luke couldn't readily identify. German, he decided. Or something close. Luke was crossing the street to the emporium as she spoke to Macky. In Luke's hands was a flyer he'd just torn down from the dress shop wall.

"Good . . . good morning, ma'am," Macky said.

"You're doing quite a good job in sweeping these steps."

"Thank you, ma'am."

It was obvious to Luke that Katrina had detected Macky's simplicity. She talked to him in the light tone one would use with a small child. "Is this your store?" she asked.

"My . . . my uncle's store, ma'am."

"Oh! And you work for him?"

"Yes, ma'am. I . . . I sweep and such. My name's Macky. Macky Montague."

"And you're quite good at sweeping." She approached Macky, reached out, and patted his shoulder. The bashful young man was taken aback, and looked over at Luke as if pleading for help.

So far Katrina had shown no indication of being aware that Luke was behind her and watching. Luke slipped closer and heard her say to Macky, "Your uncle, I'm told, is quite a wealthy man. Is that right, Macky?"

"I don't know what that means, ma'am. Wealthy."

"It means rich. That he's got a lot of money."

"I reckon he does, ma'am. He was a railroad man for most his life. He run the railroad."

"So he drove a train? Like an engineer?"

Macky laughed, amused by the notion of his uncle wearing an engineer's cap and physically operating a train. "No, ma'am. He run it like he runs this store. It was *his* railroad."

"Well! Then certainly he must be a man of fortune! Tell me, young man, what is your name?"

"I'm Macky, ma'am. What's your name?"

"You may call me Miss Haus. Or Prophetess Haus, if you wish."

Macky asked, "What a prophetess?"

"A teacher. Someone who helps others learn."

"Like in a schoolhouse?"

"Usually in a lecture hall or public auditorium. Sometimes other places."

"Can you . . . can you teach folks to read if they don't know how?"

She paused, silent. Luke held still, behind her and still unnoticed. She laughed softly, gently, and said, "You're a sweet young man, Macky. You remind me of my brother."

Macky was beginning to relax and enjoy being talked to by a beautiful woman, an experience he'd never had before. He didn't seem to notice she had skirted his question. "What's his name, your brother?" he asked.

"Peter. I called him Petey."

"Where he now?"

"He's . . . away. Gone."

"He'll come back?"

"He died, Macky."

Macky's eyes shifted from side to side and he swiped a nervous hand across his mouth. "I can't be your brother, but I can be your friend, if you want me to," he said.

She didn't answer at once. Luke had the impression of a cunning mind at work. Which roused suspicion. A beautiful woman, exhibiting friendliness to a half-witted innocent, asking him about family wealth and playing to his inevitable shyness and awkwardness while clearly seeking to engage his sympathies . . . this woman merited keeping an eye on for reasons beyond being pleasant to look at.

"How very sweet!" she said. "A woman such as I am, living and traveling alone, is always in need of friends, Macky. The right kind of friends, ones who are kind and friendly and helpful and can be trusted. I think you might be that kind of person. I can usually tell. So yes, maybe you can be my friend in this town."

"Yeah, ma'am. I'll do that. If you be my friend, too."

"Macky, I can be your friend in ways you may not even know about. All it takes is a little bit of money and a private place. I can make you feel . . . *good*. Make you very happy in ways I'll bet no one has done for you before."

Luke wouldn't hear more. He understood what she was getting at even if the innocent Macky didn't, and he wasn't going to stand by and watch some conniving prostitute try to get her hands on Montague money by taking advantage of the simplicity of a man with a boy's mind.

Luke took a step closer to the woman and deliberately rattled the flyer in his hand. Katrina heard it, turned, and looked closely at Luke. Her eye drifted down, she saw his badge, and suddenly her face blanked and she seemed to withdraw.

"Ma'am," Luke said, touching the brim of his hat.

"Sir," she replied, curt. Her eye seemed drawn to his chest to study his badge. His was drawn to hers for other reasons.

"Ma'am, I think you may have dropped this," he said, holding up the flyer he'd torn down from the wall. He'd come up with this pretext for interruption when he'd noticed just now that the papers in her hand were other copies of this same flyer. She was going around town putting them up.

"Oh, I'm quite sorry," she said, reaching to take the flyer from his hand. But he pretended not to notice her effort and drew the flyer back to read it.

" 'Prophetess Katrina Haus, Seer of Visions, Practicioner of Mediumship (Authentic) and Communicator with the Departed. Lecture and Communication to be held on Tuesday, Wiles Exhibition and Lecture Hall, Seven o'clock in the evening. Admission Seventy-five cents, Payable at Door.' "

"Yes, sir," she said sweetly in her pleasant Germanic accent. Her hand flashed and suddenly she had snatched the flyer from Luke's possession and added it to the stack in her other hand. "Thank you for returning my flyer to me, sir," she went on. "There is, I trust, no problem in my posting these notices in public places? I inquired in the town hall after arriving in your lovely town, and was told how to proceed with such a thing within the bounds of town law."

"You did the right thing, then," Luke replied. "Plenty of folks don't bother even to inquire. They just do what they want and hope to get by with it."

"I strive to be a law-abiding citizen," she said, smiling and putting her hand out for a shake. Luke took her hand and noted how it felt like a small, easily crumpled spring leaf in his own bigger paw.

"I'm Acting Marshal Luke Cable," he said, finding himself hoping, as all men do when encountered by feminine beauty, that he was making a favorable impression upon her. Never mind that she was likely a traveling harlot here to take advantage of any man she could, and a probable fraud medium besides. She was stunningly beautiful and Luke was having trouble getting past that.

"She my new friend, Luke," said Macky. "She says I make her think of her brother."

"That's . . . fine, Macky. But remember it's always good to try to get to know something about a person before you tie in too closely with them."

"Why, Marshal, what have I done?" asked the woman in frail, faux little-girl innocence. Luke caught himself thinking she'd probably perfected that juvenile voice in the company of men perversely appealed to by such a thing. It actually annoyed him.

"I take it you are this 'prophetess' who will be speaking?" Luke asked.

"I am."

"She nice, Luke," Macky said. "She not a bad lady."

"He's right, you know," she said, still with that charming smile. "I'm not a bad lady. I'm a gifted woman who can bring happiness to others by letting them speak with their departed loved ones."

"I'd like to talk to you privately for a moment, ma'am," Luke said, and her smile dwindled. She quickly forced it back into place.

"Excuse me, Macky," she said, patting his arm. He giggled.

Macky went back to his sweeping and Luke led Katrina out onto the street, directly in front of the emporium. "How can I help you, Marshal?" she asked.

"I need to ask you a question or two about your activities in Wiles," he said. "Difficult questions," he added, conscious of how delicate this would become if he proved to be wrong in his suspicions.

"Activities? Whatever do you mean, sir?"

Luke glanced around to make sure Macky and any others who might come around were out of earshot. "Miss Haus, I have been told by witnesses that men have been seen frequenting your room at the Gable House throughout the small hours of the night. Do I need to spell out my concern?"

There was a long pause, then: "Sir, I am . . . I am *shocked* at your allegation!" But her effort to sound offended came off hollow.

"No intent on my part to offend, ma'am. There's also no intent to stand by and let laws be violated in a flagrant manner, especially those affecting the morality of our community. Which is why I have to inquire."

"Marshal, I am in town to help those who have lost loved ones regain contact with them through the principles and practices of spiritism. It is for those purposes only that individuals have come to my hotel chamber."

"At two and three in the morning? And all of them men?"

"The fact that here my visitors have been men, sir, is coincidence. In other towns I am sometimes besieged by mothers seeking to make contact with their lost children, often sons killed in the late war. Other places, such as here, my clients happen to be bereaved fathers and widowers. Most times there is a mix. And I expect that will be the case after I've had opportunity to advertise my offerings more openly, which is why I've visited your local printer and had these broadsides created. I'm placing these across town. I assure you, Marshal, my activities in Wiles are of the highest and most decent nature, intended only to bring new joy to the joyless, hope to the hopeless, and communication to those who have been cut off from their dearest ones."

"You've given that little speech more than once, I think," Luke observed.

"This is not the first time I've defended myself against misunderstanding and false accusations."

"You keep conducting your business at such odd hours, and in such a setting, and such accusations are going to happen."

"Marshal, it has been my experience that some spirits will communicate with the living only in the darkest hours of night, and in settings of privacy. It is often essential for me to conduct my visitations at these 'odd hours' you mention."

"Might you consider going to your customers instead of having them come to you, then?" he countered. "Appearances, you know. A woman visiting a house with the full family present, even at a late hour, would strike folks a lot different than when a man pays call on a woman alone in a hotel room in the midst of the night. Especially one who—forgive me, ma'am—dresses herself to such display as you do."

Katrina thrust up her nose and gave a disdainful *harrumph* worthy of Clara Ashworth. "Sir, I possess the attributes I possess. I did not choose them any more than you chose those overlarge ears."

Luke squelched an impulse to put his hands up to hide his largish ears, which always had been an embarrassment to him.

"Marshal, are you through with me? I would like to go on about my business without further interference, if I may."

"Go on, then. But, Miss Haus, please be aware that I will be watching you."

She smiled and moved in such a way as to make her bosom bounce. A man on the far side of the street walked into a hitch rail. "Marshal, I am quite accustomed to being watched. I hope I gave no offense regarding your ears, by the way."

"Forget about it."

"I'll bet you wish *you* could forget them," she muttered.

She turned and headed up the steps toward the emporium front door, swaying her hips a little more than necessary beneath her long dress. Traffic on the street stopped until she was inside the emporium and out of sight.

CHAPTER SEVEN

A skittering at the rail on the east side of the staircase made Luke turn his head just in time to see a small, familiar figure come over the handrail. This was Oliver Wicks, one of the most unusual individuals in Wiles, and possessor of a unique heritage.

"'Ello, Luke!" Oliver said in a decidedly British accent, winking and grinning in a worldly way that belied his young age of twelve years. Then, typical of him, he darted up the stairs and slid through the open front door of the big store with the silent ease of a shadow dancing across a wall.

Luke shook his head in mild amusement. He knew young Oliver well enough to know what was probably luring him inside the emporium. Youthful though Oliver was, he was sufficiently precocious to appreciate feminine beauty as much as an older lad would. The scoundrel of a boy was sneaking into the emporium to ogle Katrina Haus.

Katrina Haus. Something about the woman unnerved Luke and filled him with suspicion. That whole "communication with the dead" business in particular. Why did that nag at him so? He was struggling to make a mental connection he couldn't complete.

It came to Luke that the arrival of Oliver Wicks might be fortuitous. Oliver was a boy of insatiable curiosity, interested in the goings-on of the town, whether his business or not. And because of a quirk in his heritage and upbringing, he had ways of finding answers that often evaded those in the adult world. More than once Luke had taken advantage of information Oliver had provided him. At least three minor local crimes had been solved partially because of intelligence provided by the always-snooping boy.

The quirk in Oliver's heritage was the background of his widower father, a native Englishman named Philip Wicks. Wicks, a busy and talented carpenter in Wiles, was known across the county for his agility in clambering about on the framing lumber of unfinished houses. He had applied his athleticism in a different manner in younger days back in England.

Philip Wicks had been a "second-story man," breaking into and robbing homes by employment of superior climbing ability. The criminal career he'd pursued as a young London man had grown out of his childhood activity as a "climbing boy" and "budge," a lad who was able to clamber into houses and the like and open them on the sneak to allow burglars to enter after dark. Rumors around Wiles had it that he'd left England to avoid prosecution that would have put him into incarceration for much of his life. Luke had heard the stories but had no interest in old crimes committed in a distant country. As long as Wicks remained a law-abiding citizen of Kansas, the law of Wiles would leave him alone.

Luke had never seen evidence that Wicks had continued any criminality on this side of the Atlantic, but one remnant of his past was obvious: his son, Oliver, had inherited his father's climbing skills, love of high places, and interest in the world of rooftops, balconies, and rails. Every citizen of the town was accustomed to seeing young Oliver balancing like a circus athlete on hitch rails, swinging like a monkey from rafters, tightroping his way dangerously down the ridgelines of high roofs, or leaping across deep alleyways from one rooftop to the next.

Most of the townfolk took an accommodating attitude toward "Oliver the Climbing Boy," as he was usually designated. He was an oddity, a conversation piece, a sort of town mascot made all the more interesting by the trace of British accent he'd picked up from his father.

But there were some in the town who held a low view of Oliver Wicks. They saw him not as a colorful and unusual point of personality in their town, but as a misbehaving and potentially dangerous boy driven by base and criminal impulses.

"After all, Deputy," Clara Ashworth had once said to him, "the boy has been caught looking in windows. And not windows anyone could look through, but ones only he can reach. He watches people, that vile creature does. Watches them through windows they never would imagine anyone could reach. God only knows what that boy has seen!"

There was some exaggeration in her accusations, Luke realized . . . but only some. Oliver indeed had been caught looking into second- or third-floor windows, twice at Gable House Hotel and once at the house of Bill and Beatrice Parmalee, who lived between Wiles and the little outlying community of Doggett. Beatrice had accused the boy of attempting to watch her change clothes, but no one had believed that. The woman weighed well over two hundred pounds and had a face and shape fit for a grizzly. Even the most lewd-minded boy would hardly wish to inflict upon himself the sight of her in a state of undress.

Luke had believed that the real reason for Oliver's peeping in that instance was not Beatrice, but the fine collection of rifles and shotguns Bill Parmalee had on private display in the upper room into which Oliver had been caught peering. It was a collection worth seeing, and everyone who knew Oliver knew he loved guns and had already begun his own collection. Once questioning of Oliver vindicated Luke's theory, all that came of that peeping incident for Oliver was a good scolding from Ben Keely, a milder one from Luke, and a hide-tanning from Oliver's father. Luke's only serious worry about that entire incident was that Oliver might have been eyeing the guns in anticipation of stealing one or more of them, but that never happened. Bill Parmalee retained all his guns, and Beatrice retained, and even seemingly coddled, her conviction that she had been victimized as an object of boyish lust.

Luke headed up the stairs toward the emporium door. Then he remembered something and turned back toward Macky, who was just finishing his sweeping. "Macky, could I ask you about something?"

"Yeah, Luke. Yeah."

"Upstairs, up in the attic above the store . . . is there somebody staying up there these days?"

Macky's face drained of color. His eyes darted and he swallowed hard, seemingly unable for the moment to form words.

"What's wrong, Macky? Did I ask something I shouldn't have?"

"They . . . they . . . they ain't nobody up there, Luke! Ain't *nobody*! That's where we store things and such that we got to get out of the way. Why you think they'd be somebody up there?"

"Sheriff Crowe saw somebody looking out of the window up there. Seemed pretty sure about it. Man with a beard, he said."

Macky shook his head violently, eyes squeezed closed. "No. No. No."

"Why are you speaking so . . . *firm* about it, Macky?"

Macky moved close to Luke and spoke in a tense whisper. "I don't want to get in trouble . . . not supposed to talk about it, Luke."

"Your uncle?"

"I told you . . . ain't *nobody* up there! No uncle, no nobody! Why you think my uncle's up there? What uncle?"

"What I meant was, is it your uncle Campbell you'll be in trouble with if he catches you talking about this?"

Macky slowly nodded. "Yeah."

"All right, then, Macky. We don't want to get you in trouble. So we won't talk about this."

Macky smiled, relieved. "You a good one, Luke!"

Luke smiled back reassuringly and patted Macky's shoulder. "It's good to help each other out," he said.

Luke proceeded on up the stairs and into the building. As always when he entered Montague's Emporium, Luke marveled that such a fine business existed in such a small and humble town. As general stores went, this compared to most as a mansion to a shed. Tall, broadly constructed, lined with shelves high enough that it required mounting a ladder to reach their tops. And on those shelves was an array of merchandise ranging from basic farm and ranch tools through ladies' sewing notions and fabrics, all kinds of guns and munitions for the menfolk, plus saddles and other tack gear. There were socks and leggings, canvas work trousers, and dresses fit for weddings. Shoes, boots, fencing supplies, leather goods, broaches, snoods, chairs, saws, lamps, candles, axes, saws, billiard tables, rope, chain, buckles, canned food items, cured hams, sacks of feed, tablets, and pencils . . . and out back, in a pen, chickens, turkeys, and ducks. The fowl were, like the front steps and porch, largely the responsibility of Macky, and he cared for his birds with devotion. He'd been known to softheartedly set some of them free at times, creating a small but noticeable population of free-ranging domestic fowl on the streets of Wiles.

Luke heard the muffled voice of Campbell Montague coming from the rear of the store, where he kept a large but simply furnished office. As Luke made his way in that direction, he rounded the end of a shelf and stopped.

Atop one of the rolling ladders used to access

high-shelf items, Oliver Wicks was perched, peering through the partially open glass transom above the office door of Campbell Montague. Luke opened his mouth to accost the boy, but Oliver noticed him and gestured for silence. Oliver's brashness angered Luke, but before he could speak, Katrina Haus's voice came through the closed door at an unexpected volume, the voice of a woman upset.

The door of Montague's office flew open and Katrina emerged in a rush, pretty face twisted in seeming anger and perhaps fear. She pushed past Luke, jostling him into the ladder, which in turn jostled Oliver at its top. Montague came out after her, slowly, saying, "Ma'am . . . ma'am, please do not be angered at me . . . there are reasons you cannot know for my hesitation . . ." Then he stopped, seemed to deflate a little, and leaned back against the frame of the door. His gray old eyes lifted to Luke.

"Hello, Marshal Cable."

"Hello, sir." Then, up to Oliver, "Boy, come down from Mr. Montague's ladder!"

Only as Oliver came down did the merchant notice him. "Well, son, I didn't realize you were there! Best not to climb those ladders without me knowing. I'd feel responsible if somebody fell and got hurt."

Oliver grinned. "I'm the most steady-footed fellow in all this county, sir, in this state! I can very nearly climb a straight wall if I have to, and run from one end of this town to the other without ever leaving the rooftops! And ne'er a slip or fall, ever!"

"He's telling you straight on that, sir," Luke said. "This boy is an ape, a monkey. He was taught to

climb by his father, who back in England was . . .
well, never mind that."

"A climbing boy and second-story man, a budge,
a burglar's assistant," Montague said, nodding. "Yes.
I've heard that tale. I find it remarkable and laud-
able that Mr. Wicks has so thoroughly reformed
himself and become quite the productive citizen.
Your father is the finest carpenter I know, son. I've
made use of his skills in this very edifice. Those
shelves behind you . . . he made them."

"I know," Oliver said. "And he did work for you
up in your attic not long ago."

"Uh . . . yes. So he did."

"Well, that's interesting, and might answer a
question I've been puzzling over," Luke said. "Somebody told me recently that they'd seen somebody
looking out of that attic window at the front of the
store. Man with a beard. And since Oliver's daddy
wears a beard and was working up there, maybe
that's who they saw."

Montague still had the smile he kept on his face
almost perpetually for the sake of the buying
public, but it seemed to Luke that it faltered now.
Luke remembered Macky's panicky reaction and
reluctance to address the issue of the attic's possible
occupancy, and wondered just what this delicacy
was all about.

Montague, seeming to want to shift the subject,
turned to Oliver, leaned down a little, and said, "And,
young man, what were you needing to get from the
top shelf up there?"

"Oh, sir, I don't need a thing," Oliver said. "I was
just up there for a better view."

Montague looked perplexed. "Nothing to see from up there except the same thing you see from down here. Same shelves, same walls."

"Oh, there was something to see a minute ago that ain't here to see now."

Montague still looked confused. Luke nudged out a foot and kicked Oliver's ankle just hard enough to hurt.

"One moment, please," said Montague in a suddenly choked voice, disappearing back into his office. As soon as the door clicked shut, loud explosions of coughing erupted on the other side, coughing to make it sound as if the victim might expel his own lungs. Luke frowned at Oliver.

"Lord, that's a bad cough he's got. He been that way long?"

"Just lately," the boy replied. "Last four, five times I've been in here, I heard him coughing like he has the consumption."

"I hope it's not that." On the other side of the door, the coughing continued, but a little less intensely and a little slower. "You and me got something to talk about while we've got a private moment here," Luke said to Oliver. "I think you know what it is."

"Yeah, I know. You're mad at me for looking at that woman while she was in there talking to old Montague."

"First off, a boy your age ought not call him 'old Montague.' It's disrespectful. Second off, you're right. You shouldn't have been peeping and listening in to a private conversation. And you ought not to be following any woman around just to look at her in a lusting, bad way. You know all this already."

"I do know. Sorry. She's just so pretty, that's all."

"You've got yourself in an odd and bad pattern, Oliver. You've become known as the boy who spends his time climbing on the rails and rooftops . . . but that's just the odd part, not the bad part. The bad part is this thing of you peeping at people through windows. Women in particular. There are folks in this town who believe you might be the kind to grow up and be a danger to women. Do you know what I'm getting at here?"

"Yeah. I know." Oliver's face was a portrait of dejection. His eyes shifted toward the door of the emporium again and again, a boy ready to bolt.

"I have half a mind to let you spend a little time in my jail, Oliver, young though you are. I'd lock you up and turn Dewitt loose on you. You know what he'd do?"

"Preach religion at me."

"That's right! Preach it at you right through the bars. And you know Dewitt: he wouldn't let up. No matter how much you wanted him to. He'd shove Bible at you hard and steady until you were praying to God that he'd go away. You want to spend a couple of days like that, Oliver?"

"No. Bloody hell, no!"

On the other side of the door, Campbell Montague seemed to be regaining some control of his cough. He still hacked loudly and wetly, but the explosions were less violent and steady.

Oliver declared, "I don't care what people say about me in this town—"

"You make that obvious by the way you behave," Luke cut in.

"Half the stories people tell about me looking in windows and such aren't true, Luke. Bloody lies."

"Which means the other half *are* true," replied Luke.

"Jiminy Christmas, Luke, window-peeping isn't something I set out to do! I like to climb, that's all. And sometimes when I climb I find myself able to see in windows, and some of the things I see grab me attention."

"So you look."

"Yes. Wouldn't you? Tell me true, Luke. If you were up on the porch rail of Joe Keller's house, and you looked over and realized you could see right between the curtains of his daughter Rachel's room, and she was in there getting ready for her Saturday bath, wouldn't *you* look?"

"That would catch the eye, no doubt. Anyone's eye! But it would also remind me that I was where I wasn't supposed to be, and that I'd be in a mess of trouble if I got caught. And then I hope I'd have the good sense to get down from that porch rail and back home where I belonged. And maybe find something better to do with my time than climb all over houses and fences and porches and such where I could get myself in trouble. Maybe even shot. Have you ever thought about something like that happening, Oliver?"

"No. People here know me. Nobody here would shoot me."

"Listen to me, Oliver: not everybody may have the forgiving attitude toward you that you think they do. And there's new people coming into Wiles all the time. People who don't know you and who might not take well to a local boy who talks like a foreigner peeping through their windows whenever he gets the notion."

The boy frowned, blustered a little, then said, "All right, I admit it. I like to see women. I was looking through the transom just now because from up there I could see her chest right clear while she argued with Mr. Montague. She wears that dress cut bloody low in front."

"You should be ashamed of yourself."

The boy nodded.

"Hey, could you tell what she and Mr. Montague were arguing about while you were spying on them?"

"Couldn't hear well enough. But he had one of her flyers in his hand, looking at it and frowning, and then he shook his head and that's when she raised her voice to him. Something about him being wrong about who she is, and how dare he say such a terrible thing? That's when you started shaking the ladder and she got up and stormed out."

The door opened. A weary-looking Campbell Montague, at last cough free, emerged. He glared briefly at Oliver, then forced a smile at Luke.

"You need to see me, Marshal Cable?"

"May I sit down with you in your office and us talk a minute or two?"

"I'm available to our local law enforcers anytime, Mr. Cable. Do come in."

CHAPTER EIGHT

When Montague pulled a wooden box from a drawer and from it produced an expensive cigar that he trimmed and handed toward Luke, the lawman didn't decline. Montague came around the desk with matches in hand and held out fire from which Luke lit up. Rich, tasty smoke filled his mouth deliciously. Montague lit up a cigar for himself.

"A beautiful thing, a good cigar," said Montague, blowing a perfect smoke ring that floated up toward the transom window through which Oliver Wicks had been spying minutes before.

"Yes, sir," replied Luke. "Speaking of beauty—"

"Oh, yes," Montague cut in. "I thought you might be coming to ask me about the young woman who visited here earlier."

"In a way, yes. Though initially, sir, I didn't come in specifically to talk to you. I was merely following the woman, and this is where she happened to go."

"An eye for feminine beauty, you possess?" Montague asked with a grin. But beneath the grin was something different. He seemed preoccupied, maybe worried.

"It's not beauty I'm following, though she's got aplenty of it," replied Luke. "It's a little different than that. Ever since Katrina Haus showed up in this town, I've had suspicion regarding her."

"What might that suspicion be, Marshal?"

Luke opened his mouth to answer, but a scuffling noise from high outside the door caused him to look back toward the transom window, still tilted open. Through it he saw Oliver Wicks, back up on his perch again, spying as before. Luke would not answer Montague's question with the boy within earshot, not unless he wanted Oliver spreading what he said all over town. He glared up through the glass at young Wicks and held silent.

Montague, noticing, assessed the situation, rose, and with a long rod made for the purpose, pushed the transom window closed. He grinned through the glass at Oliver as he did so.

"There, Marshal," Montague said. "If we speak softly we should be immune to eavesdropping." Montague sat again, and sighed. "I must confess I like that boy, nosey and troublesome as he may be. I'm delighted by that British way of speaking that he inherited from his father. And his mode of moving about this town intrigues me. I've seen him go from roof to roof with the agility of a leaping deer. The heights belong to young Oliver."

"Yes, sir. And in his own mind, so does the notion that he can look through any window he might happen to reach and intrude himself into any private situation he wishes simply because he is able to do so. I know he's peeped at women sometimes. I'm weary of giving the boy warnings. Before long I'll have to take more drastic actions. But I don't wish to, because I like the boy, as you do."

"I see your predicament, Marshal. Now to the matter at hand. You were following the beautiful Prophetess Haus because you hold some suspicion regarding her."

"I am confident that the woman is a soiled dove, sir, a fallen frail." Luke glanced again toward the transom window; Oliver had vanished now that he could not hear their conversation any longer.

"I am not surprised to hear that, Marshal, given the woman's way of, well, displaying herself. A merchant knows that what is conspicuously displayed is usually for sale. But she has other tricks up her sleeve, too. She came to me asking permission to hang a flyer on my public board up front, advertising what can only be a sham: a spiritualist exercise in which she claims to be able to speak to the dead loved ones of those who will pay to attend."

"You don't believe in such things, I take it."

"Highly skeptical, to say the least, highly skeptical." He paused and looked serious, then cleared his throat and set off another coughing spell, though not as severe as before. Luke watched him with concern as he struggled to recover.

"Your cough worries me, sir. Have you had it investigated by a physician?"

"Too many cigars, that's all." He pushed one of the Haus flyers toward Luke. "Have you seen these?" Montague asked.

"I have."

"She has been hanging these about town. Though she asked permission, I did not allow her to place this within this establishment. And not merely because I disbelieve in spiritualism."

"I might know what you are thinking, Mr. Montague. Perhaps some suspicions beyond what we've already discussed?"

There was a long pause. Then Montague said, "Labette. The past trouble over in Labette County?"

Luke nodded. "Do you think it really could be?"

"Several similarities are there. A pretty woman, accented voice, claims of being able to talk to spirits. Marshal Cable, can I trust you?"

"Of course you can."

"I will tell you something, then, that I would prefer to keep secret from the town at large."

"Now you've got me bewildered. But I try to keep secrets when asked, unless keeping the secret goes against my duty to enforce the law."

Montague weighed that a moment. "Good enough, then." He sat down on his desk chair again and leaned forward on his elbows. "Marshal, are you aware that I have a brother?"

"I know Macky is your nephew, and shares your surname, so I presume his father is, or was, your brother. But I have been told somewhere along the way that Macky's parents are dead. Perhaps I was misinformed. Is Macky's father the brother you are talking about?"

"No, no. Macky's father was my brother Theo, dead now since Macky was too young for him to remember him. And Macky's mother died giving him birth. No, the brother I am talking about is still living. His name is Simon, and he is my senior by three years. We have not advertised his existence in the last several years, at his own instruction. He stays to himself and does not seek the company of others. Though sometimes I think he gets lonely."

Luke made a leap. "Mr. Montague, is Simon living in the attic area above the emporium?"

Montague gaped. "How did you know?"

"I didn't. But it's been mentioned in town that a face has been seen looking out the window onto Emporium Street. I heard it said that the face resembles your own, but bearded. And when I questioned Macky about it a few minutes ago, he got worried about me asking. I take it he's had it hammered into him that he isn't to talk about the attic of the emporium. And he didn't talk about it. Just storage space up there, he told me."

Montague nodded. "Macky is saying what he's been told to say. There is a reason for secrecy."

"So I would assume." Luke waited for more explanation.

Montague puffed his cigar and coughed again. "Simon will never be a part of regular society again. He is . . . damaged, you see. Not like Macky is damaged, from birth, but from a terrible injury that was done to him a few years ago . . . some of that very 'trouble over in Labette County' you mentioned."

Luke pondered it and put it all together. "Wait . . . are you saying he was one of those injured in that inn?"

"He was. He was lucky to survive, even luckier to escape afterward. His head was crushed, you see, his brain damaged. Another traveler in the place got him out of there and found a physician. Simon survived, but at a cost. Since that time he has been unable to bear anything but the most limited human company. Strangers or difficult situations can cause him to fall into a deep and ruinous panic."

"That's a sad story, sir. I regret his misfortune."

"You would regret all the more if had you known him prior to his injury. He was a remarkable, intelligent, articulate man. It was Simon, far more than me, who brought the Montague family into the railroad industry. Simon, whose wisdom and skill led us to our success. I was simply privileged to follow the trail he blazed and to reap the benefit of his work, and to try to fill his shoes when he became unable to continue. You must know, Marshal, that as far as the world is concerned, Simon Montague is dead. Dead of massive apoplexy for these many years now. We managed to get the story into the newspapers. There is even an empty grave in Missouri with his name on the stone."

"But he is not actually dead, just hidden away in the attic of this building."

Montague nodded. "Precisely. And he is determined to remain so."

"He bears a resemblance to you, Simon does? But wears whiskers?"

"Indeed. Obviously it was Simon's face that has been seen at the window. I must urge him to be more cautious, and perhaps install a darker glass to better hide him when he looks out onto the world he can no longer be a part of." Montague frowned. "How much can he be asked to bear? After all that's been taken from him, is he to be expected not even to freely enjoy his one link with the world outside: his small window?"

"Oliver Wicks said his father, Philip, has done

some recent carpentry work for you upstairs. Does Philip know about Simon?"

"No. I hired Mr. Wicks to make improvements to Simon's quarters. But he never knew of Simon. I told Wicks I had a guest coming to stay temporarily in the part of the building he was working on, and that I wanted a livable space upstairs to accommodate him, and also in case I should ever hire a resident manager for the store. In the meantime I had already sneaked Simon out and lodged him in a hotel in Hutchinson, and hidden evidence of his prior occupation of the space upstairs. I joined Simon by the end of his first day in Hutchinson, leaving Mr. Wicks to complete the work I'd asked him to do. He did not fail my trust. He did a fine job of improving the living space. When Simon returned he was delighted with it. But Simon's stay in Hutchinson had stirred some restlessness in him. I suspect it was after that that he began looking out his window with less caution than would have been prudent."

"Why are you telling me this? I've not known before that anyone was living upstairs. Is there a particular reason I need to know now?"

"I'm rather embarrassed to tell you."

"Embarrassed?"

"Marshal, Macky had a dream. He saw the town devastated, buildings destroyed, the emporium in ruins. And apparently, in this dream, he found Simon's corpse in the rubble."

"So you believe this dream was some kind of prophecy?"

Montague shook his head and relit his cigar,

which had gone out from inattention. "No. I'm not a superstitious man. But Macky's dream made me realize that for the sake of Simon's safety, in case this place should catch fire or be damaged in a storm, it is important that someone besides me and Macky should know about him. Someone trustworthy and with a degree of authority and credibility. When you showed up today, I knew the time was right for me to share the secret in a limited way."

"Why limited? Perhaps that secret should be revealed at large. It would save a lot of confusion caused by people seeing a face peering out of a window in what is supposed to be an empty attic."

"Simon would never give his consent for a general revelation of his existence. And it would rouse some concern on my part, too: the people who hurt Simon in that inn in Labette County are still alive and on the loose." Montague's face went hard and he held silence for five seconds. "One of those people, I believe, may even now be in this very . . . never mind. I should not make speculative accusations."

"If it makes any difference to you, sir, if you're implying what I think you are, I've had the same suspicion. But I'm reluctant to broach the matter openly for fear of generating hostility and even violence that may be misplaced. That kind of thing has already happened in other places, travelers and strangers being wrongly suspected of being part of that family of fugitive murderers."

Montague nodded and puffed out another smoke ring. With the closed transom window reducing the air circulation in the room, the ring merely hung in the air over Montague's desk, slowly dissolving into empty atmosphere.

"Ah well," Montague said, rolling his shoulders. "Ah well."

A man with a large scar down the right side of his stubbled face sat astride his big black horse with the ease of one accustomed to long riding. His shoulders had an easy slump and his belly the slight bulge of middle age, but nothing about him suggested softness. His shoulders were sufficiently broad to appropriately platform the boulder of a head that filled his wide-brimmed hat. His shoulders looked like smokehouse hams inflating the sleeves of a very faded blue shirt.

The man shifted in his saddle and was glad to know that he was now within two miles of the town of Wiles. He knew nothing about the town except its location and reputation as a generally mild kind of place. No wild cow town, this one. He would have preferred it otherwise, but when a man was trying to find someone, he had to go where that someone could be found.

If Wiles didn't offer much by way of excitement, at the very least it would have a hotel and a bed. And surely a saloon or two where a man could have a drink and enjoy some solitude.

It didn't much matter, anyway. He didn't anticipate being in this town for long.

As he grew nearer the town, he began to notice the occasional house, some far away, others nearer the road. He passed one house whose yard fronted directly against the roadside, marked off by a picket fence painted milky white. As he rode by, an aging woman stepped out of the front door onto the porch. He smiled and tipped his hat in her direction and she smiled back in motherly fashion. "Beautiful evening, sir," she called.

"Indeed, ma'am." On impulse, he pulled his horse to a stop. "Ma'am, if I might ask, am I on the right road to reach Wiles?" He asked merely to generate conversation. He already knew the answer.

"Yes, sir," she told him, and he had a strong impression she was staring at his scar. "You'll be there in a very short time."

He touched his hat again and nudged his horse back into motion. He'd hoped for a supper invitation—he could smell chicken frying from inside the house, and the woman had on a kitchen apron—but no such invitation came.

He was in view of the eastern side of Wiles when he saw a flyer on the side of a telegraph pole. He rode over and scanned it, then tore it from the pole, read it more closely in the last dusky light of the day, and muttered, "I'll be damned! This may prove easier than I thought!"

He folded the flyer and put it into the inside pocket of his vest, then rode on.

Part Two
Dead Outlaws

CHAPTER NINE

That night, Luke Cable's sleep was restless, filled with distressing dreams.

In the worst of the nightmares, he was riding through a rainy dusk across Kansas flatlands, weary and eager for food and rest. He saw and approached a small, lonely house with a sign advertising meals. He rode toward it, though some voice in his dream consciousness warned him to ride on. He did not heed the voice.

He then saw himself seated at a table, his luggage beneath the table and between his feet. He was the only diner in the restaurant, if such the simple room with a bit of rough furniture could be properly called. He was seated with his face toward the front of the house, his back nearly against a filthy and oddly stained curtain that hung from ceiling to floor.

A plate of food was set before him and he began to eat. From behind the curtain came shuffling, whispering sounds, and the clump of a footstep. In the dream, Luke began to turn and look behind him. The curtain bulged toward him and something heavy and tremendously hard struck him brutally atop the head, sending him pitching to the floor, blood and brains spilling. In the dream, Luke saw himself dead on the floor. He watched wretchedly as his corpse drained, quivered, and settled, then looked up to see Katrina Haus standing in the corner of the room, smiling as she watched his death.

"Might you have a dead loved one you wish to speak with, Marshal?" she asked in her bell-like Germanic voice.

With that, the dream vanished and Luke Cable of the real world awakened and stared breathlessly at the ceiling above his bed, welcoming the realization that what had just happened was nothing but nocturnal imagination. Even so, he reflexively reached up to gingerly touch the top of his skull, half expecting to find it cracked open like a dropped egg. It was whole, uninjured. His respiratory paralysis passed and he sucked in air as if he'd just run a mile.

The rest of the night passed with little sleep. Each time Luke dozed off he found himself back in that Kansas prairie inn, hearing the noises behind the stained curtain and knowing what was going to come next. So he mostly lay awake, shunning dreams. He mentally listed the oddities of recent days to keep his mind occupied and awake.

He'd never encountered such a flurry of strangeness: a mysterious severed leg beside a railroad track—not only severed, but impossibly mummified; an unusually beautiful young woman coming to town and promising to communicate with the dead relatives of locals, while meanwhile practicing the old and dishonorable profession of prostitution;

an injured old man living in the attic of the emporium, hiding from the world the shame of his impairments; a traveling town marshal who had gone off to Kentucky and then seemingly vanished from the earth . . .

"Well," Luke said aloud to the night, "with things this strange, at least it's not likely to get any stranger any time soon."

He stared across his bedroom and hoped it was true.

Around dawn, he was very nearly asleep again, but his rest was broken prematurely by the persistent hammering of a fist against his front door. Luke rolled over, swearing softly, then got out of bed and pulled on his trousers.

Dewitt Stamps was at the door, apologetic for having disturbed his boss at such an early hour.

"Luke, there's something I need to tell you," he said. "It's Ben Keely. I think he might be back in Wiles."

"Come on in, Dewitt," Luke said, suddenly alert. "I'll make us some coffee."

Dewitt concentrated on his coffee with the same intensity he once reserved for alcohol. After two cups and meaningless chatter about everything from the death of a local dairy cow to the need for a good window washing at the jail, Luke put Dewitt onto track.

"Why do you believe Ben is back?"

"I seen him."

"What? Where?"

"Just outside of town. Near the jail, yesterday

about half past four in the afternoon. I went to go to the privy and seen him through that gap in the trees. Riding, he was."

"What did he have to say for himself?"

"Never got to talk to him, Luke. He was riding t'other direction and I don't know he ever seen that I'd seen him."

"You didn't holler at him?"

"I was going to after I got done in the outhouse, but he was gone by then. I know I should have hollered at him quick as I seen him, but the outhouse couldn't wait, you know what I mean. Besides, I was surprised to see him, and I figured I'd best wait until I could see him better to be sure."

"You saw his face?"

"Uh . . . no. But it was Ben's horse, I'm right sure."

"Right sure. But not full sure."

"Well . . . no."

"Ben's horse has nothing about it that would make it easy to recognize from any distance. From fifty feet away it looks like a hundred other horses you see in this town."

"I know." Dewitt stood and paced. "But the way this fellow sat his saddle, the way he wore his hat, everything about him, it just made me think it was Ben."

"Let me think through this, Dewitt. Ben left for Kentucky by train. He took his horse with him on the stable car so he'd have it to ride when he was in Kentucky. So assuming that really was Ben you saw, that means he came back, got his horse off the train's stable car, and saddled it up. He wouldn't do that just to ride to the jail from the train station,

Dewitt. Too close. He'd just put his horse in the livery and walk over here."

"Well, I figured he was going home and would come around into town later."

"Tell you what, Dewitt, let's check. You and me, we'll ride out to Ben's place and see if he's there."

Luke enjoyed the ride, largely owing to amusement at getting to watch Dewitt's locally famous means of transportation: a large, aged mule that, for reasons known only to Dewitt, was named Eric the Mighty. The beast was slightly arthritic, limped, and was prone to make loud, threatening brays at all who came too near—all but Dewitt, anyway. The animal seemed to hold Dewitt in great affection. Everyone in Wiles County knew Dewitt and his mule.

Eric was doing well today, stepping gamely along with Dewitt firmly rooted on his back. "I don't believe Eric is limping as much as he used to," Luke said.

"Yeah, he's better," Dewitt replied.

"You've been praying for him, right?"

"I have. But I didn't want to say that because I didn't want you laughing. Ought not laugh at praying."

"I wouldn't laugh," Luke said. "I think your prayers might have helped that old mule. Something surely has."

"Lord loves mules, too," Dewitt said.

"I'll take your word for it, Dewitt."

They rode westward, to where the Kansas flatlands gave way to a more broken and hilly region. It was in this terrain, in a small, lonely farmhouse, that Ben Keely lived his bachelor existence while serving as Wiles town marshal.

"We just going to ride down to the house?" Dewitt asked.

"Let's get up on that little woody ridge south of Ben's place and have a look from there. We can probably tell from there if somebody's been about the place."

"You don't believe me when I say I seen him, do you!"

"I figure you saw somebody, but I still can't believe Ben would have come back and not looked me up right away."

"All I can tell you, Luke, is that it sure looked like Ben. Mostly the way he carried himself, sat the saddle, and wore his hat kind of turned down toward the front. You know what I mean."

"That does sound like Ben."

"It *was* him, I tell you!"

With horse and mule tied off to trees, the two men slipped through the grove at the top of the sloping ridge until Ben Keely's small farmhouse came into view. They watched it silently for several minutes, but there was no evidence of movement or life. At length, though, something moved in the breezeway of the barn that sat near the house. A small-framed figure emerged, and Luke squinted and looked closely.

It wasn't Ben. It was Jakey Wills, a boy who lived with his family on a ranch that adjoined Ben's small piece of property and who also happened to be the little brother of Jimmy Wills, desk clerk at the Gable House Hotel. Jakey had been recruited by Ben to feed, while Ben was away, the three stray cats that Ben allowed to live under his porch. That Jakey was still doing so lent support to the notion that Ben was not in fact back in Kansas. Luke said as much to Dewitt.

"I seen what I seen," Dewitt replied stubbornly.

"Let's go down and ask Jakey if he knows anything."

Jakey, distracted by his efforts to lure a recalcitrant feline from beneath the porch for a pan of milk-soaked bread, did not see the two lawmen riding down toward the house. When he realized they were there, he bumped his head soundly while trying to get out from beneath the porch. The cat he'd been trying to lure followed him but ignored its food and raced around the house to the barn.

"Ow! I felt that clean over here, Jakey!" Luke said as the boy rubbed his injured head. "You didn't break skin, did you?"

"No . . . don't think so." Jakey examined his hand for blood and found none. "Howdy, Luke. Dewitt."

"Didn't mean to startle you, son," said Luke. "Dewitt and me were just riding out this way and I wanted to check and see if you'd heard anything about Ben getting back."

"He's *back*?"

"Well, Dewitt believes he caught a glimpse of him the other day. But he was looking through some trees and never really saw his face. The horse looked to be Ben's, or it least one just like his."

"If he's back, he ain't come around here," Jakey said. "I been coming every day and bringing scraps to these danged cats just like he wanted me to. But

I'm tired of it, and what he paid me before he left wasn't enough to cover me still taking care of these cats for all this time."

"You're a good boy to do it, Jakey," Dewitt said.

"Thank you, Dewitt. How's Eric the Mighty doing?"

"Still pokey, but he's making it. Ain't limping so much as before."

Luke said, "I kind of know how you're feeling about Ben, Jakey. I've been left doing a job for longer than I expected, too. I was looking for Ben to come back weeks ago."

"Yeah. Hey, Luke, is it true what my brother told me?"

"If it's something Jimmy said, there's no telling. What was it?"

"He says that Kate Bender is in Wiles, living in the hotel and pretending to be somebody else."

Luke raised his brows. It was the first time that anyone had spoken aloud the name he and others had been talking around and thinking about for the last little while: Kate Bender. Hearing the name said out loud knocked him back to his nightmare of sitting in that prairie inn before a stained fabric curtain. He shuddered and hoped the other two did not notice it.

"Who's Kate Bender?" Dewitt asked.

"You haven't heard about the Bender family, Dewitt?" Luke asked.

"I think maybe I've heard the name. But I don't remember nothing about them."

"They was bad, bad people, Dewitt," said Jakey. "Lived over in east Kansas, in Labette County. Old man and his wife, plus a son and a daughter. Daughter's name was Kate. Real pretty woman, by all accounts. They say she was the heart of the family and the one who led in the crimes they did."

"Robbers?" Dewitt asked.

"Yep, and worse. Killers."

"They get hung for it?"

"Nope. They got away, that's what they done," Jakey continued. He was growing into his story, speaking with increasing energy. "They was killing folks who came to a little inn they was running in a house out on the flatlands. Bashed folks in the head with a big hammer after they'd set them down to eat with a curtain behind them. The son of the family, he acted kind of half-witted, they say, but he'd be behind that curtain, and when Kate or one of the others would give him a signal, he'd bring that hammer around, right through the curtain, and smash in the brain of whoever was at the table. Kill them dead. They'd drop them down through a place in the floor into a pit, and finally they'd clean out their pockets and such, and bury them outside somewhere."

"Jakey is telling it correctly, based on what I've heard," Luke said. "A lot of the details of how they did it didn't come out until after the neighbors of the Benders got suspicious. But the Benders saw what was coming and managed to get away. A search of their place, and some digging, uncovered corpses and such."

Jakey cut in and took over the story again. "All kinds of folks started looking for the Benders then. The law, hired detectives, and just regular folks.

Whole posses of men. But nobody's caught them yet, not that anybody's proved, anyway."

"That's right," Luke said. "It's surprising. They must have divided up to avoid drawing attention. But you'd still think that, with so many folks hunting them, they'd have been found by now. Or at least some of them."

Jakey chortled. "Well, I've seen the woman who my brother says is Kate Bender. Saw her on the street in town. It looks to me like she can get a lot of attention all by herself."

"She's a beauty," Luke said.

"What did she say when you asked her if she was Kate Bender?" Jakey asked.

The question embarrassed Luke because he'd been struggling with a feeling of neglected responsibility regarding that matter. "I haven't asked her yet," he admitted. "You got to be careful about how you go about such things. There's such a hate for the Benders in this state that you don't want to make people start thinking that some particular person is one of them, not if you don't know for sure. As a peace officer I have to be careful what I say. There's been false accusations regarding the Benders made in other places, innocent folks accused because they look like them, have the same kind of German accent, that kind of thing."

Jakey said, "People are believing this woman is a Bender all on their own, Luke, whether you say it or not. Hell, I believe she's one of them!"

Luke sighed, closed his eyes, and shook his head. "I'm going to have to talk to her about it, whether I want to or not. I guess I'd hoped she'd just disappear, go somewhere else. Or that Ben would come back all at once and she'd be his problem, not mine."

"Luke, whether she's Kate Bender or not, she's still breaking the law," Jakey said. "My brother says men are coming into the hotel and visiting her room in the middle of the night. I'm guessing she ain't up there telling them stories about Baby Jesus."

"Well, she was at church last Sunday," Dewitt said. "I seen her going in the door of the Methodist church with my own eyes."

"Well, as I've heard it told, Kate Bender was a churchgoer at the same time she and her kin were murdering the patrons at their inn. Presented herself as a good Christian woman. All to make folks trust her." Jakey paused and chuckled. "Kind of funny, in one way. A murdering woman who also whored herself and claimed to talk to folks' dead loved ones. Twisted as a wagon spring, that is! Can you think of anything more loco?"

"It's wrong to try to talk to the dead," Dewitt said. "Bible teaches that."

"Be that as it may, after the war was done, there were a lot of folks who got interested in talking to the dead," Luke said. "You can't much hold folks at fault for wanting to talk with, say, a son who got shot down in battle."

"That don't make it right to do, though," Dewitt countered. "Bible teaches it's wrong to dally with familiar spirits."

"The point is that the fact there were so many dead opened the door for frauds and fakes like Kate Bender, or Katrina Haus, or Prophetess Katrina Haus—all of which may be one and the same—to get their hands into the pocketbooks of bereaved people."

Jakey shook his head. "I don't know that such things are always frauds. My old granny talked with her dead forebears all her life . . . and sometimes she knew things they'd told her, things she couldn't have knowed otherwise. Things they'd seen folks doing, because they were ghosts and you didn't know they were there watching. I got in trouble for stealing my uncle's knife when I was just little. The ghosts seen me do it and told Granny, and Granny told Pap on me."

"I don't know that I believe in ghosts, Jakey," said Luke.

"Maybe it was Ben Keely's *ghost* I seen," Dewitt said. "Because, I swear, I seen *somebody*."

"I'm sure you did, Dewitt. I just doubt it was Ben, dead or living. He wouldn't come back to Wiles and not come to his own house. And he wouldn't hide himself from his old friends. I'm sure of it."

"Hey, I can't tell you where Ben Keely is," said Jakey, "but I can tell you law gents where you can find a whole passel of bad outlaws."

"Can you, now?"

"Sure can, Marshal. And they'll be easy to catch."

"How so?"

"They're all dead. And some of them are just pieces."

"What the hell are you talking about, boy?"

Jakey shrugged and grinned. "It ain't far, just on down the railroad track a ways. Want me to show you?"

Luke, though suspecting that the boy was playing them for fools, said, "Why not?"

It took a few minutes for Jakey to run back home, saddle up his horse, and rejoin the group at Ben's house, but soon the boy was leading the small group of riders westward along the tracks, Luke all the while wondering if this were all a waste of time.

"So tell me about this 'passel of outlaws,'" he said to Jakey.

Again the youth shrugged. "It's a train, or a couple of cars, anyway. They're parked at the old side track, got awnings and tents and lanterns and such strewed around. Kind of a stage platform built up there, too."

"Why?"

"'Cause they're show cars, I reckon. Pay your money, see the show."

"Show . . . like dancing Gypsies or something?"

"Funny you should say that," Jakey replied. "There is a Gypsy-looking man around them cars. And one of the signs says something about 'Gypsy Nicholas Anubis, Preserver of the Dead.'"

"What the hell's an 'Anubis'?"

"I don't know. Just somebody's name, I reckon."

Luke rolled his eyes. "And I thought things couldn't get any more strange than they have been lately."

CHAPTER TEN

Lying on his belly on a brush-covered ridge that overlooked a small creek, and beyond it, a railroad track, Luke squinted and tried to read the signage attached to the two railroad cars parked on the side track below. One in particular intrigued him for what he thought it said, but he was unsure of his reading at this distance. He wished he had the pair of field glasses that at this moment were in one of his desk drawers back at the office in Wiles.

"You've got young eyes, Jakey. Can you make out what that sign says down there?" Luke pointed.

Jakey replied, "It says, 'Professor Raintree's Outlaw Train and Chamber of Criminal Relics.' And the other one over there, it says, 'Traveling Cabinet of Infamous Preservations,' and then 'Gypsy Nicholas Anubis, Preserver of the Dead.'"

"I can read *those* signs, Jakey! It's that smaller one, that white one over on the front car, that I can't make out."

Jakey looked hard, but shook his head. "Can't read that one from here, either. I'll get closer."

Before Luke could respond to stop him, the boy vaulted forward and down the slope. There was no sign of life around the two sidetracked railroad cars. Jakey scrambled athletically down the incline and dropped behind a bit of brush. Luke watched him lift his head and study the sign.

Just then something moved below. Luke caught sight of a man coming around from the far side of the end-to-end railroad cars. The man did not look up the slope, did not see those who hid there, watching him.

He was strangely dressed, in a bulky, flowing shirt cinched around his waist with a cloth sash, and with some sort of odd headgear. He was carrying a heavy hammer in his right hand, and walked to the outside corner of a tent that stood near the railroad cars. He knelt and began hammering a wobbly tent stake, tightening the rope support and making the tent a little straighter.

"Why's he dressed that way?" Dewitt asked in a whisper.

"Don't know," replied Luke. "Maybe that's Gypsy Nicholas. Or Professor Raintree."

"What kind of thing is this?"

"It appears to be a traveling museum of some sort," Luke said.

"What's an 'infamous preservation'?" Dewitt asked.

"Couldn't tell you, Dewitt. No idea."

"Should we go down there and bust this thing up?" asked Dewitt.

"No grounds to do so that I can see. Nothing criminal about operating a cabinet of curiosities that I know of. There's things like this all over . . . this one is just different because it's on rails and wheels."

"Then why did we sneak and hide like this?"

"Because of Jakey talking about there being a 'passel of criminals.' I wasn't sure what we'd find, so I decided we should do this on the sneak. Let's get back to town now. There's nothing illegal about a traveling show. My gut tells me to leave this be for now."

The man below bolstered the rest of his tent stakes and went around to the back of the railroad cars again. As soon as he was out of sight, Jakey scrambled back up to his companions, and the three of them went back to where they had left their horses, mounted, and rode back toward the empty house of Ben Keely, missing town marshal.

Jakey and Dewitt were in a mood to talk, while Luke was content with silence. He kept apart from the other two as they rode, leaving them to chatter at each other while he softly whistled an old fiddle tune. When they reached the point where Jakey would take his leave of them, Luke and Dewitt said farewell and rode on together toward Wiles as young Jakey went back to his home. The sky was clouding over, the air beginning to feel thick and moist.

At the edge of town, Luke suddenly stopped his horse and exclaimed softly, "Blast it!"

"What's wrong?"

"Dewitt, Jakey went down that hill so he could read what was on that sign, then he plumb forgot to tell me what it was, and I forgot to ask."

"Luke, Jakey tried to tell you, but you didn't hear him over your own whistling."

"So what did it say?"

They were riding into town now, already in sight of the jail.

"Jakey said it said something about a 'new dis-hun,' or something."

" 'Dishun.' New edition. Or addition, maybe?"

"Yeah, that was it! 'New addition: the crumbled skull of Big Harpe the murderer.' That was what Jakey said, or something close. I don't know who Big Harpe is, though." Dewitt paused. "Why you frowning like that, Luke?"

"Because I *do* know who Big Harpe was, and I know whose family has owned his skull bone for years. Ben told me about it. And I have to wonder how that jar could now be in the possession of some traveling railroad show when it was something Ben Keely went back to Kentucky to fetch."

They dismounted. The sky was terribly overcast by now, darkening the day and giving it an ominous feel.

Hardly had boot heels touched the street before an out-of-breath Oliver Wicks launched himself down from the low, flat-topped roof of the jailhouse and landed catlike on the dirt, startling Luke, Dewitt, and their horses.

"What the hell, boy!" Luke exclaimed. Then: "Sorry about the cussword, Dewitt."

"Marshal, you got to come now!" Oliver said, gasping. "Sheriff Crowe just got himself shot dead over at the Redskin Princess! *Dead!* And some of the folks have got the fellow what done it tied up in a storeroom, and they're talking about hanging him!"

As Kansas prairie towns went, Wiles had fewer than the average number of saloons, and those that did exist were of good quality and, owing to lack of

gambling and dancing girls, didn't attract the row-
dier element that had rendered infamous some of
the rougher dens and dance halls of Dodge City and
other cattle towns. Which was why the grim news
delivered by Oliver was hard for Luke to believe.
Oliver pummeled him with details of the story as
they trotted along street and boardwalk on their
way to the farther side of town.

"It happened fast, they said. No sign it was coming. The sheriff had come in the saloon after the
first fellow was already there, the one with the scar
on the side of his face. By this time Scar-face was
drinking beer and eating a sandwich. Sheriff Crowe
went over to him straightaway, they said, and sat
down like maybe he'd come in specifically to see
this man. The two of them talked a bit, just quiet
talk, and everybody else went on playing billiards
and so on, paying no attention to them. Then, all at
once, the man with the scar leapt up and pulled out a
pistol he'd been carrying hidden beneath his jacket,
and Sheriff Crowe was shot through the chest before he was halfway out of his chair. Someone said
that the bullet went right through his badge. Well,
that shot didn't kill him, so the sheriff still went for
his own pistol and had it out in his hand before
Scar-face shot him the second time. This one right
through his brow. Needless to say, that one killed
him."

Leaving Dewitt behind on the pretext of tending
to the jail, although it was at present empty, Luke
went on toward the Redskin Princess, mind reeling
at the thought that he had an actual shooting death

to deal with. And the victim the county sheriff, no less. He was more nervous and overwhelmed than he would want to admit. He'd always supposed that, in the case of a murder, the first thing he'd do would be to call the more experienced Sheriff Crowe in to assist and guide him. He'd never envisioned a situation in which Crowe himself would be the murder victim.

A milling, excited crowd remained outside the Redskin Princess; the electric tension of their emotion made the atmosphere crackle. As he reached the fringe of the clot of people, Luke began to be noticed, eliciting a mix of responses. He heard mutterings that said it was about time the law showed up; he heard others that bewailed the arrival of a man with a badge because what was needed here was a good quick hanging without interference from the law.

Luke pushed his way through the cluster of humanity and entered the saloon. As he did so he learned that the sense of electricity in the atmosphere was not generated merely by the tension of the situation and the crowd. A sudden flash of lightning filled the sky, followed by a bolt of thunder that made the ground vibrate and the saloon walls shudder.

Luke strode through the saloon, stepping around overturned chairs and accidentally kicking strewn glasses and bottles here and there on the floor. It had been an atypically rough night at the Redskin Princess, it appeared.

"Over here, Marshal," said a man on the east side

of the room, near a table that had been scooted to one side. Luke walked over.

"That's where he lay," the man said, pointing to a circle of blood clotting on the dirty floor. At the edge of the circle were bits of fleshy matter that Luke guessed was brain. He felt queasy for a moment.

"So there's no question that he's dead, I guess," Luke said to the man.

"None. The bullet went in his forehead and took the back part of his head with it when it came out."

"Where is Sheriff Crowe's corpse now?"

"Wilton Brand had him carried over to the undertaking parlor. He signed off on the death papers."

Luke was just about to ask the man where the shooter was being detained when a shout from a back room gave him the likely answer. He headed in that direction, reaching protectively for the butt of the Colt revolver holstered at his right side.

Three burly men had the prisoner in an otherwise empty back room; a man Luke had never seen before, yet who roused a sense of possible familiarity. He had apparently just made a bolt for the door and was reaping the consequences from his self-appointed captors. Luke froze for a moment, aware that this was the most difficult and precarious situation he had faced in his young career as a peace officer.

"Town marshal!" he bellowed, drawing his pistol. "What's going on here?"

One of the men had the prisoner in a headlock, and looked squarely at Luke. "We got you a murderer here, Marshal. Murdered Sheriff Crowe, he did. Shot him right through the head."

"I've heard. I'll take custody of that man now."

"No, sir. If we let go of him, he'll make a break for it, and he might just get past you, pistol or no pistol."

The speaker was John Bailey, local blacksmith, one of the strongest men in Wiles County. Though Bailey was known as a good citizen, Luke never much liked him because Bailey so obviously did not respect him. Bailey believed that officers of the law should be men of fist and muscle, and was frequently vocal, after a few beers, in declaring that the slimly built Luke Cable was not cut out for the role he played in Wiles, any more than Ben Keely had been. Bailey's opinion carried much less weight than his frame did, but Luke was annoyed by it nonetheless. He'd heard rumors that Bailey had once approached the town fathers to seek the marshal's appointment for himself, but Luke didn't know if that was true, nor did it matter, because Bailey's bid, if it had ever happened at all, had not been taken seriously by the local powers.

"What's your name, man?" Luke demanded of the scarred man.

The prisoner struggled and ignored the question. Luke drew closer and spoke louder, repeating his query.

The man stopped trying to fight his way free. He panted, relaxing, glanced down at Luke's badge, then stared at Luke. "Howdy, Marshal."

"I asked your name."

"Wesson. Ed Wesson." The man began to struggle with his holders again.

"Fairly believable alias, friend," Luke said. "Most

just come up with something like Joe Jones or Bill Smith."

John Bailey said, "You're right about it being an alias, Luke. You know who this man really is?"

"Why don't you just tell me, John?"

"Because you're the lawman. You should be able to figure it out yourself. Take a look at him!"

Unsure what Bailey was trying to make him see, Luke eyed the struggling prisoner. The burly man was a stranger, yet that earlier sense of something recognizable about him lingered.

The man turned his head and the scar on the right side of his ruddy face throbbed lividly. And at that moment Luke knew, or at least strongly suspected. An image from a year-old wanted poster flickered in his memory.

" 'Scar' Nolan?" he said.

Bailey nodded vigorously. "You should've figured that out right off, being law. If I was marshal, I'd not have to have been told who it was."

"Yeah, you're a treasure, John. A real treasure."

"Well, here's some advice you can treasure, lawman. You'd best deputize me and these boys right now, or else I doubt you'll get this old boy to the jail without him getting away from you. Scar Nolan didn't get famous for escaping the law by being easy to hold."

"I ain't no Scar Nolan!" the prisoner growled, struggling. "Honest to God, lawman! My name is Ed Wesson."

"Shut up, you!" Bailey ordered.

"Bailey, it's you who should shut up," Luke said. "As much as you don't like it, I'm the marshal here."

"*Acting* marshal," Bailey corrected. "Acting like a marshal without being one."

"Bailey, I don't know why you hold as deep a grudge against me as you do, but it's nothing but a nuisance to you and me both. I'm officially appointed to fill in for Ben during his absence, and if the town had wanted you in that position, they'd have put you there. But they didn't, and you being jealous over it don't change that."

"Oh, listen at him preaching from his speaking stump!" Bailey mocked. "Ain't you proud to be took in by such a fine man of the law as this one, Scar? Not that he had nothing to do with it. It was me and these other boys who got you!"

"I'm telling you, this is a damned mistake!" the prisoner declared, struggling harder. "I'm no criminal!"

And suddenly he was free. A wrench and a twist, and by seeming luck he found a way to get out of the grip of the men holding him. He lunged away from them and toward the door, sending him directly past Luke.

He didn't get far. Luke had his pistol out and swinging before the fellow had completed his first step. The heavy Colt caught the scarred man on the left temple and drove him down to the floor. He crumpled and quivered and passed out, groaning a curse as he did so.

CHAPTER ELEVEN

Bailey continued his gibes, and Luke continued to ignore them, as they carried the unconscious prisoner to the jail, drawing a lot of attention from the citizenry as they went. But all the way there, Luke increasingly suspected that Bailey was right about the identity of the prisoner. Scar Nolan, one of only two surviving members of what had been a group of four train- and bank-robbing brothers from Missouri, was famed for his lethal hatred of peace officers and for his ability to escape custody, sometimes by sheer luck, more often by magician-like skill. And if this really was Nolan, it might explain why Sheriff Crowe had approached the man to begin with, and why things had turned violent.

Luke caught himself wondering if Dewitt would be up to the task of keeping watch over a clever man such as Scar Nolan was reputed to be. He'd escaped jail, according to one story, by knocking out and changing garments with a preacher who had come to visit prisoners.

When they reached the jail, Dewitt was not in the front office, and the front door was locked. Luke opened it, calling for Dewitt and getting no answer.

"Where's your jailer?" Bailey asked.

"Can't say," Luke replied. "Outhouse, I guess."

"Or out drunk somewhere."

"Dewitt don't drink no more."

"Ha! Yeah. I reckon."

Luke eyed Bailey and wondered why the man was so determined to dislike him. Sometimes, it seemed, there were situations in which two particular people just couldn't mix together without something dramatic happening. Vinegar and soda.

Just then they heard Dewitt's voice, calling from behind the door that divided the front office area from the block of cells in the rear.

"Dewitt?" Luke called back, putting his hand to the door and pushing it open.

Dewitt was indeed in the cell block, in fact in one of the cells, barred door closed and locked, imprisoning him. He was seated on the cot that served as the cell's bed, leaning back against the stone wall. He looked up glumly at Luke, then past him and through the door, where Bailey was visible, holding fast to the scar-faced prisoner. The other men who had helped transfer the prisoner had already quietly vanished, apparently seeing their volunteer duties as completed. The prisoner was Luke Cable's problem now.

Luke let the door close and went over to the cell to face the glum-looking Dewitt.

"Dewitt, what the devil?"

"It . . . it was an accident, Luke. But I think God caused it for my own sake."

"God locked you up in your own jail. Yeah."

At that moment the sky opened up, driving rain and even more lightning and thunder, and Luke wondered if there was some kind of divine message in the timing of it. If so, he couldn't decipher it.

"I'd come back here to pray, Luke. Had to do it. I was feeling tempted, tempted bad."

"Liquor?"

"I'm ashamed of it, but yes. Hardest temptation I've had since I put the bottle aside. It was all I could think about . . . I nigh went out the door and out to get liquor, and all I could do to keep myself from it was come back here and pray. But when I threw open the door to the cell and came in, I slung it too hard, and it bounced back closed behind me. And locked itself. And I'd left the key out on the desk. But being locked in kept me from having a chance to give in to the temptation. And I believe I would have give in if I'd been able to get out of here. It scares me how close I was to letting the demon grab me again, Luke."

"We can talk about that later, Dewitt. Right now we have a prisoner to deal with."

Out in the office, Bailey cursed loudly as his prisoner made another lunge for freedom, which Luke turned just in time to see. Bailey responded quickly to the effort, fist coming up in a blur and pounding the scar-face man on the left side of his head. The man fell straight down, as if his legs had gone soft, and clumped heavily on the floor. For a moment Luke thought the man was dead, but then he groaned loudly.

Luke went out and knelt by the man to reassure himself further that he'd not just witnessed a violent death in his own office. Sure enough, the man was breathing, but with eyes limply closed, showing their white undersides through slitted lids.

Bailey was cursing and shaking the hand he'd just hit the man with. "Did you break it, Bailey?" Luke asked.

"Don't . . . think so. But it feels like lightning-fire running through it." Another violent shake of writhing fingers.

From his desk, Luke picked up the key to the cell that held Dewitt. He went back and freed his deputy. In the front office he said, "Dewitt, help me get this man on the floor back into that same cell you just left."

"What's wrong with him?" Dewitt asked.

"Bailey just busted him in the head for trying to escape."

"You a deputy now, too, Bailey?" Dewitt asked.

"Just helping out," Bailey replied. He wasn't shaking his hand anymore, just massaging it gently with the other hand.

"Is this the man who shot Sheriff Crowe?" Dewitt asked.

"It's him."

"I think I know who that is, Luke. I seen his picture on a notice. I think that man might be Scar Nolan."

"I think so, too. So does Deputy Bailey."

" 'Deputy Bailey'?"

"Well . . . by that I mean, he's acted as a deputy by helping bring in this outlaw."

"Helping?" Bailey said. "Hell, seems to me I was the one who done the whole job! I was the one who brought him down after he did the crime, and held him, and kept him from getting loose. I did a hell of a lot more than just 'help' you get him down the street to the jail, Marshal! And if there's a reward due on this fellow, I'll not let *you* cheat me out of it!"

Luke, feeling the annoyance that Bailey always roused in him, held his tongue long enough to let him, Bailey, and Dewitt get the unconscious man into the cell. By the time Luke locked him in, he was groaning more loudly and beginning to come to. Lightning turned the glass-and-bar cell window into a flashing light.

"You reckon he is Scar Nolan?" Dewitt asked.

"He could be. Right now we don't really know. But in a way it doesn't matter. Whoever he is, Nolan or Wesson or anything in between, this is the man who killed our sheriff, so he's here to stay for a good while."

Dewitt looked very somber. "Something wrong?" Luke asked him.

"I'm . . . I . . ." Dewitt clearly had something to say, but could not get it out. He flicked his eyes in the direction of Bailey, and Luke got the message.

"We'll talk in a minute," Luke said to his jailer.

With the prisoner now securely locked in a cell, Luke turned to Bailey. "How's the hand?" he asked.

Bailey was gently massaging his fingers. "Hurts. But I don't think it's broke."

"You don't need a doctor, then?"

"Nah. Nah. I'm fine." Bailey looked through the bars at the slowly recovering, wakening prisoner. "He might, though. I jarred him pretty damn hard."

Nolan/Wesson gave a well-timed groan.

"Could I ask you a favor, then, Bailey? Not that you ain't already done more than most."

"What?"

"Would you go to Doc Artemus's place and fetch him back here?"

"Why don't you send your jailer there? Why make me your errand boy?"

"Dewitt and me have some talking we need to do. This is the most serious case we've encountered since he became jailer. I need to make sure he understands how important it is to keep this prisoner secure at all times. Especially if he does prove out to be Scar Nolan. Nolan, they say, has escaped more jails than a fox has fleas."

"All righty. I'll go fetch the doc. And, Luke . . . I know you and me ain't been the best for getting along, but the fact is I'm not working right now, and if you need to hire on some help here to make sure this prisoner stays a prisoner, I'd be proud to work for you."

"I'm going to think hard about that, Bailey. And I thank you for the offer."

During the time that Dr. Artemus evaluated the state of the prisoner in his cell, Luke walked with Dewitt outside the jailhouse. Inside, Bailey was still there, helping oversee the situation.

"Why's he doing that, Luke?" Dewitt asked. "I don't trust him."

"I can't say I do, either," Luke replied. "Bailey and me have never got on well, and it's always seemed to me that he had some personal motive for anything he does."

"I bet I know what it is, Luke. I bet he's hoping the county will name him sheriff to replace poor old Sheriff Crowe."

"You think so? Because he's got no experience at all as a professional peace officer. You think they'd put somebody in like that?"

"That's the point, Luke. He's acting like a good citizen volunteer to make himself look good in their eyes. He's hoping they'll say, 'That Bailey might never have been a peace officer, but by gum he sure showed his stripes the way he jumped in and helped out old Luke Cable when Sheriff Crowe got gunned down. We ought to make him sheriff!' That's what Bailey is hoping they'll say. Betcha anything."

"You may be right. And if you are, my days as marshal are numbered. Even though he'd be county-hired and I'm town-hired, my office works too close with the sheriff for us not to get along well. He'd find ways to undercut me and try to get me out of the job. Don't you figure?"

"I do."

"But at the same time, Dewitt, I might take Bailey up on an offer he made me. He's willing to step in and be a temporary deputy for me while we've got Nolan locked up. And it is Nolan. I had a notice about him in the file, and there was a picture. It's him, hardly any doubt about it."

Dewitt reacted with an expression Luke couldn't interpret. "So Bailey's taking my job?"

"No. You'd still be jailer. Bailey would just help out on the side for a while."

"What about Hank McAdams? Why not just get Hank to help more?"

"Hank stuck a letter under the jail door, Dewitt. He's quit as deputy. His mother's nigh dead, and he's going to spend all his time for now seeing to her. Once she's gone, he's going to put cattle on the family land and do some ranching."

"So Bailey is replacing Hank."

"Sort of. Just temporary for now."

"Luke, I'm sorry to speak so forward, but this ain't a good idea. You and Bailey working together . . . that's cat and dog."

"I know. But can I speak just as 'forward' as you?"

" 'Course you can, Luke."

"Don't take offense, Dewitt, but I'd feel better having somebody like Bailey here at the jail some as long as we've got such a notable prisoner. Especially one with a reputation for being able to get out of jailhouses."

"You figure he'd get past me, huh?"

"He's a tough old bird. Cool and slick as a dog's nose. And you're still a new jailer. Yeah, I figure he might get past me or you, either one."

"But not Bailey."

"Can't say that. Maybe he could wrangle Bailey, too. But you got to admit that Bailey handled him pretty well today. As much as I don't like Bailey, he's a capable fellow. And not many private citizens would have stepped in like he did to bring down a hoss like Nolan right after he gunned down the county sheriff."

"That's true."

"Here's the way it all adds up, Dewitt. We've got a prisoner that's going to require some close care and attention. With Hank quitting we're shorthanded as it is. You're a new jailer and I'm just an acting marshal. Bailey has offered to help and he's already proven he's got some natural capability in this kind of work, just by what he did today. We need his help right now, like it or not. I'm inclined to take him up on his offer. But I want you to be with me on this, Dewitt."

Dewitt took a long, slow breath. "I don't like Bailey. I don't feel good about him coming in and strutting around the place with his smart mouth flapping like it always does. I don't like the way he disrespects you, Luke, because you've been mighty good to me and I won't hear nobody talk you down."

"Well, that means a lot to me, Dewitt. But I'm used to Bailey's attitude. And it all evens out. If he don't like me, well, I don't much like him, either."

"But you still want to make him deputy?"

"It's not a matter of 'want.' For the moment, we *need* him." Luke grinned. "Dewitt, you locked yourself in your own jail cell."

Dewitt grinned sheepishly, thought about it a couple of moments, and nodded. "I guess we do need him."

"I'll talk to him, then. Right now. I'll have to hope the town will go along with giving me a little more money to pay for the extra help."

"What if they say no?"

"They won't. I'm only asking for a short-term hire, for one thing, and I know this town's leaders well enough to be sure they aren't going to take any chances with the likes of Scar Nolan locked up in our jail."

Bailey accepted Luke's offer, with the understanding that the temporary appointment was dependent upon approval by the town fathers. Later, as Luke met over beer with District Attorney James Crandall to discuss the murder of Sheriff Crowe, Crandall, who also had always disliked Bailey, questioned Luke closely about the move and let it be known that he thought it doubtful at best.

Luke answered those doubts with a candor that surprised even himself. "It all came down to the fact that Scar Nolan is a more clever fellow than most of his ilk, if his reputation is valid. Certainly more clever than Dewitt. I've got the strongest feeling, Jim, that if I left Dewitt alone to tend the jail with Scar locked up, Scar would wrangle himself a way out of there before Dewitt knew it was happening."

"Sounds like you're questioning your own wisdom in having put Dewitt into that job, then, Luke. Maybe he wasn't up to the task."

"I believe in Dewitt. In normal circumstances, that is. But this ain't a normal circumstance. Our jail has mostly been occupied by drunks and brawlers and the like. It ain't common at all to have a murderer locked up in our jail. Especially not the murderer of a lawman. And a murderer with a famous name at that."

"No, this isn't at all common," the district attorney agreed. "I'll grant you that." He paused. "Have you noticed how it seems like nothing is ordinary or common around this town anymore?"

"Believe me, Jim, I've noticed. It's about all I can think about these days." Luke paused. "Along that same line, look at what was in our prisoner's pocket." He reached beneath his coat and removed a folded piece of paper he handed to the other.

Jim Crandall opened and examined the paper briefly. "Interesting," he said, looking up. "I've seen some of these around town, hung up on walls and poles. But I've never really heard of such a thing as this. What the devil is an 'Outlaw Train'?"

Luke said, "Dewitt and me paid a visit out to this 'Outlaw Train,' but didn't go all the way to it. We were just curious about what it was, like you are."

"Well, did you find out?"

"It appears to be a traveling show and exhibition of some kind. Something to do with outlaws and things having to do with them, I think."

Crandall frowned in thought. "This outlaw circus shows up, and then one of the best-known outlaws in this part of the country happens to ride into town and kill the sheriff. And this flyer turns up in his pocket. Reckon there's a connection between this traveling show and Scar Nolan?"

"One thing at a time, Jim. Before I try to figure out these Gypsy showmen, or whatever they are, I've got another question needing clearing up. And I'm hopeful I can maybe clear it up tonight, or get a better notion of the lay of the land, anyway."

"Going to go communicate with the dead this evening, are you, Luke? I saw that flyer around town, too."

"You got me figured, Jim."

"I've got some questions about that young woman," Crandall said. "The fact you are going to hear her lecture makes me suspect you have questions yourself."

"I do. The kind of questions you don't ask out loud unless you really know what the hell you are talking about. Because asking them out loud could get somebody killed."

So Crandall didn't speak out loud but whispered. "Bender?"

"The thought has crossed my mind."

"Mine as well. And some others here in town. And many of them are not as discreet as you are being. It will be intriguing to find out what happens when she makes her presentation this evening."

"You going?"

"I'd half go just to look at her. I've not seen such a beauty before. Just don't tell Hannah I said that."

"I'll keep my mouth shut. I'd not want to get you in hot water with your wife."

"Speaking of wives, Luke . . . when do you think you'll get one of your own and settle down?"

"God only knows. And so far He's not talking out loud, either."

"You still paying call on that young woman over near Ellsworth?"

"Haven't made the journey since Ben left town. Can't get free to do it, you know. But we write each other letters now and again."

"What's her name? I'm forgetting."

"Sally. Sally James."

"No kin to Frank and Jesse, I assume."

"Not to my knowledge. I hope not."

They finished their beers and talked a little more about innocuous topics. When they rose to leave, Crandall caught Luke by the arm. "Can't believe I haven't mentioned this yet, but you should know you're already being talked up by the county leaders as a replacement appointment for Sheriff Crowe."

"You're joshing me!"

"Not at all. I reckon they've been impressed with how you've handled your town office since Ben cut out on us. And it's not like there's a whole slew of experienced lawmen hereabouts to form a pool of candidates."

"In Dewitt's figuring, Bailey will put himself forth as a candidate for the job. Point out that it was him who restrained Nolan after the shooting, and try to ride that into office."

"I'd not have thought of that myself, but Dewitt may be right," Crandall said. "But the county won't buy that particular bill of goods, I'll wager. Bailey's got no real experience under his belt. You're the man they'll want."

"I'm not sure I want the job."

"It would be a good position for a young man such as yourself. Better pay than the town alone gives you, and respect. The kind of position a man wants in case he decides ever to turn Sally James into Sally Cable."

"Good Lord, Jim, first you got me as county sheriff and now you've got me married off! Who put you in charge of living my life for me?"

"Just trying to help an old friend find his best opportunities."

"Well then, I appreciate that. But the opportunity I want to find is the opportunity to go back to being just a simple deputy of Wiles, Kansas, working for Ben Keely. But I don't know that's ever going to happen. I'm believing more every day that goes by that something has happened to Ben. I'm afraid he's gotten himself killed somewhere, somehow."

"I worry the same thing, Luke."

They said their farewells and parted. Luke walked slowly through the streets and alleys of his town, not patrolling so much as simply letting his thoughts roam free. He wasn't looking forward to the evening's presentation by "Prophetess Katrina Haus," finding the whole spiritualism concept to be grim and morbid. But, he reminded himself, if the talk grows hard to bear, at the very least he could enjoy the beauty of the speaker.

He turned onto Emporium Street and heard the atonal singing of Macky Montague come wafting down the avenue. The swish of his broom on the emporium steps almost kept time with the song.

Luke crossed the street so he could pass the emporium without directly encountering Macky, not being inclined just now toward conversation. Sure enough, Macky did not look his way as he passed the huge store on the opposite boardwalk. But Luke did happen to glance up as he passed, and caught a glimpse of something moving behind the attic window. He strained his eyes and thought he saw a face, or part of a face, peering back at him.

Reflexively he almost waved, but didn't, not being sure that the old man living a lonely existence in that upper area would want to know he had been seen.

Feeling strangely dejected, Luke pressed on while Macky kept sweeping and singing.

Chapter Twelve

Prophetess Katrina Haus looked solemnly across the crowd gathered on the second-floor Wiles Lecture Hall, closed her eyes suddenly as if stabbed by pain, and said, "I feel the presence tonight of many spirits, many departed loved ones who wish to give comfort to those remaining behind and grieving them."

A faint, anticipatory murmur swept through the gathering. Several people scooted forward in their seats in postures of eagerness. Jimmy Wills, who had been recruited by the speaker to collect admission at the door and who had taken his seat in the back row when Haus began speaking, moved forward in his seat, too, and when he had arranged himself so as to have the best possible view of the shapely speaker, smiled. She was what he'd come to see. Let the show go on.

Haus waved her hands to signal for silence, and when the only noise in the room came from the muffled creak of a passing wagon on the street outside, the woman spoke softly, her Germanic accent thickening. "I sense that someone here grieves for the loss of one taken before his time . . . someone who died young, tragically and violently." She paused, closed her eyes again, and rocked from side to side as if swayed by a great, unseen hand. "Tell me, my people, by the raising of your hands, if you have lost a young loved one to violent and premature death!" She opened her eyes, still swaying, and raised her own hand.

Out in the crowd, hands rose . . . slowly, except for one that shot up like a bolt before Haus even finished speaking. This was the hand of Clara Ashworth, who was seated in her usual Sunday-best dress, her fancy hat held on with one of the French hat pins she had shown Luke out on the street. Beside her was her husband, Howard, who looked extraordinarily uncomfortable to be there. Luke, who was seated on a row end three-quarters of the way back in the lecture hall, recalled Dewitt's recounting of seeing Ashworth making a nocturnal visit to Haus at the hotel. Luke studied the Ashworth couple and pitied them: Clara for the secret unfaithfulness her husband hid from her, and Howard for the pain he had suffered through the loss of his only son, Michael, in the late war, a victim of bushwhacking redlegs. Michael's death weighed far more heavily on Howard than Clara, because Michael had been the product of Howard's first marriage, and though Clara always referred to him as her son, he was not in fact so. Clara had accepted the youth for the sake of convenience and familial harmony. Howard, though, had truly loved the boy. The trauma of the young man's death had led to Howard's move to Wiles from the town of Lawrence, or so everyone said. In Wiles he and Clara had settled, and being an aging couple they had borne no children of their own.

Haus took note of the raised hands and nodded. "I'm . . . I'm sensing a military connection, something to do with war and battle . . ."

Several voices rose to let the "prophetess" know that she was connecting. Clara Ashworth was visibly trembling, perched on the edge of her seat, hand still uplifted and now waving. Luke was surprised that it was Clara and not Howard who was reacting so strongly . . . until he remembered that Howard was far from likely to call attention to himself in the public presence of a woman with whom he had cheated on the wife seated by his side. Howard no doubt wished he could be invisible at this moment.

Haus's voice became singsong: "Yes . . . yes . . . there are spirits here, eager to communicate with their living loved ones, to tell them they are well, happy, joyous in the life beyond . . ."

Clara turned to her husband. "Did you hear that, Howard? He is well and happy!"

Howard, speaking more loudly than he'd intended, could be heard by most of those present when he said, "We don't know that it's Michael she's talking about, Clara. Could be some other soul."

Luke noticed that Prophetess Haus did not seem to have heard Howard, or acted as if she had not, even though Howard was seated close enough to the front that he should have been easily audible to her. Luke had heard him from several rows back.

Haus's next words made Luke sure she'd heard him after all. "The letter *M* . . . I'm sensing the letter *M* . . ."

For his part, Luke was sensing an *F*, for "fraud." It wasn't hard to see what this woman was doing:

casting a wide net in search of subtle information from the audience, and gradually narrowing it based on the responses she received. In a group of this size, particularly a group gathered for a spiritualist exercise dedicated to contacting the dead, obviously there would be many there grieving for lost loved ones. And given the reality of the war that had cost so many lives mere years before, it was inevitable that many of those lost loved ones were young, killed violently before their times. No special insights or skills on the part of Haus were needed.

"Letter *M*, did you say?" a woman on the opposite side of the lecture hall asked.

"Yes," replied Haus. "But there are others as well. . . ."

"Is there a Julia?" asked the woman, voice frantic.

"Yes. She draws nearer to us . . . Julia . . ."

"Oh, Julia!" the woman wailed, coming to her feet and looking toward the ceiling as if she expected to see Julia come floating through the wall itself. "Let me hear from you! Are you well? Are you in heaven?"

"Sit down, Amelia!" the man behind the frantic woman demanded. "You're blocking my view!"

"And lovely Miss Haus is a view not to be blocked, ain't she?" said a nearby man, too loudly, drawing chuckles from men and reproving glances from women.

The wailing Amelia didn't heed any of it. She remained afoot, cringing and crying, tears staining her twisting face. Luke watched it all and marveled at the gullibility of the human race. Luke's mind was open; he was willing to believe in communication with the dead if Prophetess Haus could clearly demonstrate it. So far she had not done so.

Haus came nearer to Amelia. "Madam, I will speak next with your Julia. Until then, there is comfort that Michael seeks to give to his family." She waved her hand in the direction of the Ashworths . . . and only then seemed to realize who Howard Ashworth was. So at least was Luke's assessment, based on the demeanor of both. Howard stared at the floor and would not look at Haus, who was momentarily at a loss for words, and coughed in what struck Luke as a deliberate manner. Luke could imagine how clumsy the situation was for her, dealing in public with a man who had made a nocturnal, carnal visit to her hotel room, and him with his unwitting wife standing right beside him.

After the moment had passed, Haus regained composure and control quickly. She stood tall, body going rigid, and closed her eyes tightly, trancelike. She began to sway slightly.

When she spoke next, her voice was different. Deeper, almost masculine. Luke was initially startled by the change, but quickly recognized that it was a practiced effect, probably a standard part of her program of deception.

"Father," she said. "Mother. It is I. It is Michael."

The crowd murmured in awe, but Clara Ashworth was not as impressed. "I was not Michael's mother, and he never referred to me as such," she said. "And that is *not* his voice."

Unfazed, Haus turned her face toward the woman, eyes fluttering partly open for half a moment. "No . . . it is my voice, but Michael speaks through me.

Though you were not his mother by birth, he valued the raising you gave him, and from the perspective of the other side, he now views you as Mother."

Clara seemed stunned and confused, and found nothing to say. Haus stepped closer to her. Luke, watching, noticed that Howard looked as if he wanted to vanish into the floor. He surely felt threatened by Haus: with one word she could reveal his tryst with her and destroy his reputation. And she could do so without revealing her own involvement, simply by passing off as information from "the other side" the fact that Clara's husband had betrayed her with another woman.

Clara spoke, weakly. "Michael sees me . . . as his . . . mother?"

Haus used her deeper voice again, just for a moment. "I do, Mother. You made yourself mother to me. You earned my love."

Clara's eyes suddenly brimmed and she raised a hand to her face. "Oh . . . Michael . . . did you hear what Michael said, Howard?"

Howard grunted and nodded, still not looking at Haus.

Clara sank to her seat again and buried her face in her hands, sobbing. Haus turned away and Howard slumped in visible relief, no doubt hoping that she was through with the Ashworth family.

He tensed again when Haus turned and looked at Clara. "He is telling me more," she said, normal voice again. "Michael is telling me more." Her eyes flicked to Howard Ashworth for a moment.

Luke heard Howard breathe a quiet "Oh, God . . ."

"Michael is in heaven," Haus said. "He is in

heaven, and he is happy. He stands with the angels in eternal joy."

Clara nodded. "Thank you, Prophetess Haus. Thank you for sharing this wonderful message. And tell Michael that he is loved, and missed. And that I am proud to be called his mother."

"He hears you," Haus said. "Your words increase his joy."

After the "communication" involving the Ashworths was complete, the pattern of the evening was established. Haus gave similar comforting words on behalf of the spirit "Julia," then spoke again to the group as a whole, cleverly moving from broad comments and questions to more narrow, specific "facts" regarding persons present and the spirits who supposedly had come to communicate with them. In each case Luke was able to trace the pattern of how she achieved this, and see that there was no mystical power involved. Merely clever manipulation and careful listening and response. The only communication going on was unwitting, drawn from the minds of the gullible believers who had come to hear the "prophetess."

In each case, the "spirits" showed up as wished, and in each case their news was comforting and positive. All were in heaven, all were happy, all were protecting their loved ones left behind and would welcome them on the "other side" when the time came. Before long Luke was realizing how effective a fraud Katrina Haus was . . . and now that he knew *what* she was, he was wondering all the more *who* she really was.

The more he thought of such things, the more unsettled he felt, the more overwhelmed by how this town, this job, this life of his was changing. Not long before, he'd been a mere small-town deputy whose duties involved, at worst, hustling drunks into a cell, rattling shop doors after dark, breaking up the occasional squabble or brawl, steering a straying child back in the direction of his or her parents, fetching horses that had strayed from hitch posts. Low-paying work, but easy, and usually safe. And always with higher-ranking lawmen in the background to carry the final responsibility if things took a turn. Now, though, he was dealing with a murdered sheriff and a prisoner in that case who seemed likely to be a noted, long-sought outlaw. Furthermore, he was seated in a public gathering at that moment, facing a woman who very well could be the infamous fugitive murderess Kate Bender, hiding behind a false identity.

For the first time since entering the law enforcement profession, Luke was wondering if he'd made an error of judgment.

Prophetess Haus was on the opposite side of the room, declaring she was getting a strong impression of a communication coming from someone whose name had begun with a *B* and who had died from "difficulties within his or her upper body," when the hallway door nearest to where Luke sat rattled and squeaked open. He glanced over and was surprised to see that it was Dewitt who had opened it. Dewitt peered shyly into the little auditorium and quickly found Luke. He signaled with his hand for Luke to come out into the hall.

Luke might have ignored Dewitt if not for the desperate look on his face and the possibility of trouble back at the jail. Though Dewitt was not on jail duty that night, that task having fallen to Bailey.

As Katrina Haus began to tell yet another family that their lost loved one was fine, eternally happy, and eager to communicate the same to those who grieved them, Luke rose and hurriedly slipped from his place and out to the hallway.

"What's going on, Dewitt?"

"You got to come, Luke. You got to."

"What's wrong?"

Dewitt seemed as though he might break into tears. "You just got to come, Luke. I don't know how it happened, except for what I could cipher out on my own."

"For God's sake, Dewitt, you're starting to make me nervous."

Dewitt didn't respond. He was already leading the way out of the lecture hall and into the street, where he walked at a fast clip toward the jail.

Near the jail, Dewitt finally spoke again. "I think it might be my fault. If I'd been in there, I could have stopped it."

Had they been farther from the jail, Luke might have physically seized Dewitt and forced him to explain what he was talking about, but it seemed more feasible at that point simply to go see for himself. But Luke hesitated to thrust himself into a situation about which he had no information.

"Dewitt, stop."

The jailer stopped and looked at Luke as if bewildered. "Luke, we got to get in there."

"Before we do, tell me one thing: is there an ongoing danger in there that we'll be walking into?"

Dewitt's lip trembled and a tear slid down his face. He shook his head. "No danger, no. It's past that now, Luke. And I think it's my fault."

Luke said nothing, but pushed past Dewitt and onto the porch. The front office window was lighted, but the jail gave forth a sense of emptiness. But that could not be, Luke knew as he put his hand to the knob, because the prisoner had to be in there, back in his cell, and Bailey had been left on duty to tend to the place.

Luke entered the office. Bailey was not there. The chair was pushed back from the desk and the ring of cell keys was not at its usual place, hanging from a hook inside the rolltop desk. The door between the front office and the cell blocks was ajar, but only a few inches.

"John! John Bailey? It's Luke! Where are you?"

No reply came. Nor was there any sound of movement back in the cell area. Luke walked to the center of the office and looked around, then noticed that the cabinet that was used to hold the personal effects of prisoners was open. And empty.

"John?"

Dewitt, who had entered the office behind Luke, said quietly, "He ain't going to answer you, Luke."

"Where is he, Dewitt?"

Dewitt's eyes cut toward the door leading from the office into the cell block area.

Luke knew almost intuitively what he would find when he opened that door, and the impulse to run away from it all was strong. But he was the marshal. He had to do it.

He went to the cell block door and pulled it fully open.

Now he knew what had become of John Bailey.

CHAPTER THIRTEEN

He was sure Bailey was dead even before a check for pulse confirmed it. Bailey's neck was twisted at a strange, extreme angle, head tilted like that of a hanged man cut down from a noose, eyes and mouth half open. Bailey lay in front of the cell that had held the scar-faced prisoner. A cell now empty.

Luke knelt beside the corpse and shook his head helplessly. "You knew when you came to get me at the lecture hall that Bailey was dead," he said to Dewitt, who stood nearby, sniffling and wiping tears.

"I knew. But I hoped I was wrong. I hoped we'd come back and he'd have got up and been all right."

"You don't just get all right from having your neck broken, Dewitt."

"Lord, Lord. It's my fault, Luke. I'm to blame for this."

Luke came to his feet and rubbed his chin while looking over the situation.

"No, Dewitt. Seems to me that it was Scar Nolan who is to blame for this. You can see what happened . . . he managed to get Bailey to come back here with the keys, and he got him close enough to the cell door here that he could reach out twixt the bars and get hold of him around the neck.

Then he reached through the bars with the other hand and wrenched poor old Bailey's neck so hard it snapped it. Bailey slumped down, dead, and all Nolan had to do was reach out, get the keys, and let himself out of here like he was walking out of the outhouse after a good squat." Luke nudged Bailey's body with his boot toe. "Damn! Damn it all to hell!" Then, "Sorry about the cussing, Dewitt."

Dewitt shook his head and kept on leaking tears. "My fault," he muttered again. "My fault."

"How is it your fault, Dewitt?"

"'Cause I wasn't in here to stop it."

"Nothing wrong with that, Dewitt. Remember: it wasn't your night to tend jail. You had no obligation to be here."

"But if I had been . . ."

"If you had been, Bailey would have been pissing mad that you were hovering around him like a hen. And what happened might have happened anyway. Or it might be you lying dead, not Bailey. You can't second-guess the Lord, Dewitt. Tonight was Bailey's night to tend jail. And his night to die."

"'It is appointed to a man once to die, and after that the judgment,'" Dewitt said, quoting scripture.

"The point is, it wasn't your fault," Luke said. "If anybody in this office ends up taking blame for this, it will be me. I'm the marshal, and I was out of the office when it happened. Out attending a fraudulent spiritualist's exercises."

"Well, you went there because there's a chance that that woman is breaking the law. And maybe that she's even a wanted killer."

"Even so, Dewitt, there'll be some folks in this

town who say I was wrong to leave the jail tended by an inexperienced jailer like Bailey."

"Or me."

"What they'd say if it had been you was, 'Luke should never have left a drunkard in charge.'"

"But I'm not a—"

"I know, I know. The point is, people still say it even though it isn't true. So you and me, I guess we shouldn't be worrying about what people say. Just what the truth really is. That's all that matters. And the truth is that what happened here wasn't your fault and it wasn't my fault. It was Scar Nolan's fault, and Bailey's own carelessness."

"Yeah. And now he's escaped."

Luke nodded and paced. "Dewitt, I got something for you to do. We have a murder here, so we need to get District Attorney Crandall. And you need to fetch Wilton Brand, too, since he's coroner. Can you do that for me?"

"I'll go get them right now."

Wilton Brand stood slowly and brushed his hands on his trousers. Turning to Crandall, he said, "Well, I think we can rest assured that there is no longer any doubt that the prisoner who murdered our sheriff and now Mr. Bailey was in fact Scar Nolan. Nolan has killed men in exactly this manner at least twice before tonight. A neck-snapping trick he claimed to have learned from a Chinaman, or so the story has it."

"How do you learn such things, Jim?" Luke asked. "You've got more such lore about the outlaw breed than anybody else I've ever known."

"Well, the first person who ever told me about

that was none other than old Ben Keely. Ben was always interested in those kinds of details about criminal folks, you know. Kind of collected them. He told me it was a habit he picked up from his father, who was a history-loving type, and even had an outlaw relic or two he'd collected."

"Well, I wish Ben was here right now to take charge of this situation," Luke admitted. "This peace officer business is turning out to be a lot more than I ever signed on for."

"It has taken a few dark turns lately," Crandall said. "This isn't the Wiles that most of us have known for so many years. 'Most peaceful town on the American prairie,' they used to call us. And now we've got sheriff murders and jail escapes and dead jailers and such. And you know, Luke, you might think a man in my position would be pleased in the secrecy of his heart to have crimes of note being committed in his district. But I'll own up right off: I don't know if I have the capacity to rightly and successfully prosecute crimes of this stature. They may be beyond the reach of a man who has spent his life prosecuting the theft of small items from store shelves and the burglary of lonely little prairie houses and the occasional 'borrowing' of a horse. I'm overwhelmed, Luke. Plain old overwhelmed! You know what I mean?"

"I know exactly what you mean, Jim. Exactly. And just now we've got another overwhelming task to do, one I have never done before."

"Forming a posse?"

Luke nodded sharply. "Forming a posse. One that can be ready to leave come first light."

* * *

It went well, in Luke's estimation. An eight-man group, all well-mounted and, thanks to the attention that Ben Keely had paid to building up a good little marshal's office armory, well armed. He had good rifles, an assortment of Winchesters and Henrys, available from the gun cabinet in the corner of the office. Wilton Brand was the only posse recruit who declined one of the weapons, preferring to use his own well-maintained Winchester, a rifle whose weight, balance, and sighting he had customized carefully and which was his most proud possession.

It was Luke's hope that no guns would be fired in the capture of Scar Nolan. With eight good men in pursuit and Nolan's lead not particularly strong, he was optimistic of a good outcome.

The posse set out as the first rays of sunlight pierced the east. Investigation and questioning the previous night had indicated the direction Nolan had fled, and the fact that he'd stolen his own horse out of the livery.

The posse pursued, though a track was hard to find because Nolan had stuck to the main thoroughfare out of town, where horse traffic was heavy in both directions and tracks tended to obscure one another. At length they found one track that seemed, by its freshness, to have been more recently laid than most, and concluded that this was probably the mark of Nolan's horse. They followed until, outside town, the track veered off the road and onto grassland.

"Looks like he's trying to throw us off," observed one posse member, Jesse Cauley.

"Always was like you to state the obvious, Jesse," said a voice Luke hadn't expected to hear. He twisted in the saddle and saw that Hank McAdams, former deputy of the Wiles, Kansas, marshal's office, had ridden in to join the group. The sandy-haired young man rode up to Luke's side and put out his hand.

"Care if I join this delegation, Marshal?" he asked as Luke pumped his hand.

"You're more than welcome, Hank," Luke replied, grinning. "I didn't expect to see you, though. How's your mother faring in her illness?"

"She rallied a good deal, just yesterday, and all at once. So when I heard what had happened at the jail—Joe Taylor told me as I was coming out real early this morning to collect eggs at the henhouse—I knowed I needed to come help you out. Not long ago, it might have been me instead of Bailey who got choked to death back among the lockups."

"Could have been you, me, anybody," Luke said. "I regret sore that it happened to Bailey. Him and me were never friends, as you know, but he seemed to truly want the chance to work for the town, and I needed him, so . . ."

"If I'd have knowed Mama would rally like she has, I'd not have left you to start with, Luke. But I swear, she was nigh on the edge of death, and the doctor said there was no hope for her. But then she just turned around, her color came back, and she got back on her food again. Miracle of God, I reckon."

"Now you're starting to sound like Dewitt Stamps," Luke said. "He's working as a jailer for me now, you know."

"Yeah. I heard that. Surprised me. I reckon I think

of Dewitt like he was, before he got off the whiskey.
But a man can change, I guess."

"I believe that Dewitt really has. He's doing a
good job for me, though he's nervous in his work.
I'm proud of him for doing as good as he has. You
want to come back to your old job, Hank?"

"I didn't figure you'd want me back, since I quit
on you."

"I need your help, and you're the best man I know
of, terms of experience."

"We'll talk about it after we catch Nolan," Hank
said. "But yeah, I think I might like to come back, if
you'd have me."

"I'll have you. Hank, Dewitt is a good man, getting better all the time, but he managed to lock himself in his own cell the other day."

Hank mulled that, and laughed. Luke laughed,
too, and was glad that Dewitt was not there to see
him do it.

They rode on, following as best they could the
path seemingly taken by Nolan.

But Nolan was not to be readily found. The posse
rode and tracked and watched, but at length it
became clear they had lost the trail. The search for
Nolan turned into a search for tracks.

After two false starts and one dead end, Luke
was nearly ready to declare the search at an end
and admit defeat. Nolan had bested him. Let some
other lawman in some other county or town capture the man.

"There he is!"

The speaker was Brand, and he was pointing toward a rise to the northeast. Luke looked, and sure

enough, a mounted figure was limned against the sky at the highest point of the rise, looking back at them.

"Wilton, let me take a look through those field glasses," Luke said.

"That him?" Brand asked a few moments later, as Luke adjusted the binocular focus.

Luke studied the distant figure intently. Lowering the field glasses, he shook his head. "It ain't Nolan, that I'm sure of," he said. "But what surprises me is who I think it *is*."

"From here, without field glasses, I would swear that was Ben Keely," Brand said.

Luke handed the field glasses back to Brand. "If you'll look at him through these, you'll find it *still* looks like Ben Keely."

Brand took a look, refocused, and looked again. "Too far away to be plumb sure, but it does appear to be him. He's back, Luke. Ben is back."

"So it appears, Wilton. So it appears."

"Should we ride up and make sure?"

"We got other fish to fry. Let's go see if we can get back on Nolan's track again." He took another look at the distant horseman on the hill. "From the look of it, though, I may owe Dewitt an apology. He might have sure-enough seen Ben Keely after all."

PART THREE

RAINTREE AND ANUBIS

CHAPTER FOURTEEN

"I don't know, Nick," said the man with the tattooed ears. "You know I'm always hesitant about being so open about what we've got. I think eventually it's going to get us into hot water, this kind of advertising."

David Akers, known now to the world by the more provocative and exotic moniker of "Gypsy Nick Anubis," smiled benignly and shook his head. "No," he said back to Professor Percival Raintree. "Never been a problem anywhere else and it won't be here. Giving folks a free taste of what we're serving only makes them more prone to part with a little admission money later on."

Raintree shook his head and put his hand in his pocket, finding the small metal flask there. He unstoppered it and took a hot but refreshing swallow. Anubis watched, eyes locked on the flask, his tongue flicking thirstily between his lips.

"You go at that flask more and more these days, Percy. You're nothing but a bundle of nerves anymore."

"I'm not easy with being here, in this particular place," Raintree returned. "We shouldn't have come here. Too great a chance of somebody recognizing him." With that he nodded toward a figure seated on the shotgun side of the farm wagon upon which Anubis sat in the driver's seat. "And now you're getting ready to parade him through town God, Nick, we're fools to be so careless!"

Nick Anubis shook his head. "Not a chance of it, Percy. He can't be recognized. Even if somebody pulls off the mask, there's no face there to be seen. You know that better than anyone. You're the one who shot it off him! I don't believe this fellow's own mother would know him from looking at the smear of raw meat that's under that mask."

"What if we've overlooked something? What if we're being overconfident?"

"Trust me, Percy. Taking Tennessee here into town isn't our problem. Our problem is that not nearly enough people are coming out to the train here, any more than they did at Ellsworth. The flyers I hung ain't doing the trick this time. People need to see more sometimes, need to get a clearer notion of what we've got to show them. That's why me and Tennessee got to go to town. When I did the same thing at Ellsworth, business picked up."

"Hell, maybe we should have just stayed there longer instead of coming here. Nick, are you sure that you aren't just going into town to find a bottle?"

"As long as you are pulling from that pocket flask every five minutes, don't you lecture me about bottles, Percival. Anyway, I'm not going into town for a bottle. I'm going to let folks get a glimpse of our dead friend here, and whet their appetites to see more of the same." A gust of wind swept through, knocking askew a hand-painted sign that was leaned up against the chest of the unmoving figure on the rider's side of the wagon seat. Nicholas paused to correct it, and also checked the stability of the wooden post that ran up against the lifeless figure's spine, keeping it upright. "I will tell you, though, that I do have another reason for going to town this evening," he continued. "How would you like to have the best display yet on the train?"

"What the hell are you talking about, Nick?"

"I'm talking about Kate Bender, that's what I'm talking about."

Raintree froze, frowning, and stared at his partner. "Kate Bender the murderess?"

"The same. The same one who fled with her murdering kin and was never found. The same Kate Bender who used to present herself as one who could communicate with spirits, and who also sold herself to men as a common whore. The same Kate Bender who is back to her same old tricks again, using a different name, and this time without her murdering family with her. No inn this time with a curtain and a hammer and a trapdoor in the floor. This time there is nothing but her dead-folk-speak and her whoring. And she's doing it in Wiles. She's a good part of the reason folks haven't much been coming to the train, I suspect. I think she's got so much attention that nobody even pays heed to the flyers and such we've put up. That's why I've got to make this run into town. And maybe, if we're lucky, I can start getting some notion as to how we might get our hands on Miss Bender. Can you start to imagine the crowds we could draw if we had

Bloody Kate Bender's corpse to show? We'd grow rich, Percy. Rich!"

"What name is she using?"

"Haus. Prophetess Katrina Haus."

"Well, yes . . . we could get rich off this Katrina Haus if she proves out to really be who you say she is, not just some other soiled dove pulling the same kind of spirit-talking confidence game that Bender did. And, of course, she'll do us no good, whoever she is, unless she conveniently drops dead and we get lucky enough to get her corpse for display."

"Sometimes that can happen, Percival. People just conveniently dropping dead and all."

"We don't murder folks to stock our corpse displays, Nick. You know that."

"Tennessee here might be inclined to disagree about that." He tilted his head toward the corpse propped up on the seat beside him.

"Our man here didn't meet his fate so we could display his body, Nick. I've told you that. He died because he refused to be reasonable. The use of his corpse as the Tennessee Kid was just a later inspiration. A way of adding value to an earlier difficult transaction."

"I'm going on now, Percival. Too antsy to hang around here. But I'll stretch it out, take my time. I don't want to roll into town until after dark. This kind of thing always works best when folks see it when it's dark."

Dewitt was unsure what drew him back again and again to the place Bailey had died, because it was to him the most hated place he knew. He would never forget the soul sickness he had felt when he saw Bailey's corpse, and the empty cell where the murdering Nolan had been.

"Dear Lord, let me forget," Dewitt prayed aloud, pacing in the narrow passage between cells. He was back to simple, basic duty again—minding the now-empty jail—but since the murder of Bailey and the escape of Nolan, the jail was no longer an easy place for Dewitt to be. "Let that picture of poor Bailey lying there go out of my mind," he said to the empty human cages around him.

He couldn't help but ponder the fact that it used to be easy to forget whatever needed forgetting. All that had been necessary was to pull a cork and press glass to lips. It was easy to forget in the days his mind was cloudy. Now, the farther he got from his last drink, the clearer his mind grew. And a clear mind was a remembering mind.

"I'm sorry, Bailey," he said softly. "I'm sorry you got killed. I hope you went to heaven."

Ten more minutes passed and Dewitt's funk remained strong. At last he shook himself, went up to the front office and there dashed a little water on his face from the wash bucket in the corner, and decided that fresh air was called for. He left the office and told himself he was doing so in order to make rounds while Luke was out manhunting. Never mind that rounds were not part of his assigned duty just now. There was certainly nothing to do at the jail except dwell on the fact that a murder had occurred there.

He had to break this morbid sense of gloom hanging around him. Daylight was what he needed. Daylight and fresh air and a bit of exercise.

Closing the jail, he paused on the porch and wondered if he was doing the right thing. Luke and his posse would return at some point, most likely, probably with a recaptured Scar Nolan in tow. Luke might be angered to find the jail closed down.

Dewitt promised himself he wouldn't stay away from the jail for long. A good walk, a brightening of the mood, and then he'd come back. Odds were he would be back in the front office before Luke even returned.

Gypsy Nick Anubis, who in the earlier days of his far-from-exotic life had been not a mysterious "Egyptian-born" showman but merely a young assistant to an Alabama embalmer who made his living giving cursory undertaking service to battlefield dead so their corpses could be shipped home for burial in family plots rather than interred in anonymous mass graves, settled himself more comfortably on the seat of the wagon and rode through the pleasant day with a dead man at his side. He was glad to leave behind for a while the Outlaw Train that provided a living for himself and his employer, Percival Raintree, a man he'd met four years earlier in an alley behind a billiard hall in Chicago, where both of them were emptying bladders filled earlier in the saloon next door. It was inside the saloon that Nick had first noticed Raintree . . . noticed his tattooed ears, actually.

The back-alley meeting had led to a surprise: Raintree already knew who he was. "I'm pleased to speak with you at last, Mr. Akers," Raintree had said while hitching shut his fly. "You'll pardon me if I don't offer to shake hands under the circumstances."

"It wouldn't much bother me to shake your hand, sir," Nick had said. "In my line of work I'm accustomed to touching that which most would shun."

"Embalming?"

"A good guess. You are correct."

"No guesswork involved, Mr. Akers," Raintree had replied. "I came to the saloon this evening because I saw you enter there. It was you I hoped to meet!"

"You followed me?"

"I've been following you for some days now."

"I don't like being followed."

"I think you'll be pleased, under these circumstances," Raintree had replied. "I'm here to offer you a marvelous opportunity. Shall we go have another drink and talk a while?"

"I'm always thirsty."

"Then let's go."

Jakey Wills had just fed Ben Keely's cats once again when he saw the wagon come rolling over the rise against the backdrop of a darkening, cloud-filled sky. He paused in the yard of Keely's empty house and squinted at the approaching vehicle. The driver was oddly dressed, in loose, flowing clothing that reminded Jakey of the garb of the man he'd seen outside the Outlaw Train the day he'd hidden on the hillside and watched the place with Luke and Dewitt. But he didn't think this was the same man.

He couldn't be so sure about the man riding shot-gun. The fellow had a sign of some sort leaned up against his chest. A mask, like a flour sack, but with no eye holes, so that his entire head was hidden.

When the wagon was close enough, Jakey was able to read the sign. He drew in his breath in surprise and awe, and stared freely at the figures on the wagon, particularly the masked one, who did not move at all.

"Hello, young man," Nick said. "What are you up to today?"

"Feeding cats."

"Cats?"

"Yes, sir."

"How many you got?"

"Three. But they ain't mine. They belong to Ben Keely."

Nick squinted in thought. "Keely. Why does that name sound familiar?"

"You've probably heard of him, sir, if you've been around these parts. He's the town marshal of Wiles, the town over that way." Jakey thumbed eastward. "Except he ain't in Wiles. He went off weeks and weeks ago to Kentucky to see kinfolk, and he ain't come back."

"That so?"

"Yeah. Hey, mister, is that honest-to-goodness the Tennessee Kid there in the seat beside you?"

"That's what the sign says, ain't it?"

"Yes, sir, but I just wondered if it's real."

"It's real. And that's him."

Jakey's face was the image of awe. He walked around the wagon and stood near the dead outlaw, looking up. "He got shot down in Colorado, right? About two years ago?"

"That's right."

"Shot in the face with a shotgun, wasn't he?"

"That's why we keep that bag over his head. Folks couldn't bear to see what's under there."

"Can I look?"

"It ain't part of our show, son. And believe me, you'd not really want to see it."

Jakey paced around, still studying the corpse. "You with the Outlaw Train, mister?"

"I am. You can call me Anubis. Nicholas Anubis."

"What kind of name is that . . . Anubis? Never heard that before."

"Neither had I, until Raintree gave it to me."

"Who is Raintree?"

"He owns the Outlaw Train. He's a smart man, Raintree."

"Why did he name you Anubis?"

"It's the name of some Egyptian god. God of mummification. And my first name, Nicholas, that's not really mine, either. It's another name Raintree gave me. It comes from Saint Nicholas, the patron saint of all kinds of workmen, including embalmers. Like me."

"Are you the one who embalmed the Tennessee Kid here?"

"I am. And the others we've got inside the train."

"The Outlaw Train is full of dead people?"

"There's a few. And parts of others. Bones and preserved hands and feet and such. And relics of other kinds . . . guns, knives, clothes, hats, boots. Folks like to see such things, you know, if they have something to do with a famous outlaw. We got the pitchfork that was used to stab the life out of Curly Drake, the gunfighter who killed that bounty hunter and his whole family. And we've got a flattened bullet that was dug out of the wall of the Blood Bucket Saloon over in Denver after it had passed through the skull and brain of Barrett Hampton, the famous hangman from Judge Shriver's court down in Texas."

"I'd like to see those things."

"Then you come see the Outlaw Train. I'll look for you there." Anubis reached beneath into a pocket on the side of his flowing, baggy shirt and produced a small card he handed to the boy. It was a pass for free admittance. On its back was, in small type, a listing of several of the associated featured attractions.

Jakey read it closely for a moment. "It says here that you have the jar with the head of Big Harpe the murderer. But that can't be right."

Anubis immediately looked nervous. "Why not?"

"Because I know the man whose family has that jar. It's the man who lives in this house here, the man who owns them cats. Our town marshal, Ben Keely."

"He went to Kentucky, you said?"

"Yep. Some time after his father died. Went back to see his kinfolk."

"Well, Percival—that's Raintree, Percival Raintree—he went to Kentucky a while back for the very purpose of finding the family who owned that relic. And he did find them. And became the new owner of Harpe's head. Or what little remains of it."

"They sold it to him?"

"We've got it, so I reckon they did. Hey, son, is your family at home?"

"Yes. Why you ask?"

"I was hoping maybe your father might have some whiskey about the place and you might share a little of it with a passing stranger."

"My pa wouldn't let me share his whiskey. But I know where somebody else's whiskey is." Jakey pointed at Ben Keely's house just beside the unmoving wagon. "There's a bottle on Ben's shelf. Only a little left in the bottom of it. But with Ben being gone I don't figure there's any reason you couldn't have it."

"You got a key to the place?"

"Ben left me one when he asked me to tend to his cats."

"Well, I don't think the Tennessee Kid here will mind sitting out here alone for a little while."

Jakey eyed the seated corpse while Anubis climbed down. "So it's true that the Tennessee Kid lost one of his legs, I see." Until just then the boy had failed to notice that the propped-up corpse indeed was one-legged, the trouser leg on the left side cut off just below the hip area and stitched shut.

"Yeah, it's true," Anubis said. "He died a hard death, that boy did. Holed up in an old farmer's house, shooting it out through an upstairs window with some law in Texas, and never did see the farmer's half-wit boy creeping up on him with the stove-wood axe. The half-wit took that leg off at the hip with one swipe. Axe was keen as a razor, so goes the story. Well, when the Kid got chopped he reared up in pain right there at the window. What he didn't know was that a Texas Ranger had managed to climb up on the roof of the porch that that window looked out onto. The Ranger jammed that shotgun through the window and blowed off the face of the Kid." Anubis paused and smiled. "Then, the story goes, the half-wit fussed at the Ranger for having made such a mess. Said his mama would holler at him for letting his room get all bloodied up."

"Huh. How'd you end up with his corpse, if that's really the Tennessee Kid?"

"I didn't. It was my partner, Raintree. He has a touch for getting hold of what he wants to find. And a knack for tracking down those who have it. I mean, he tracked *me* down, and he managed to track down your marshal's family in Kentucky, and get that Harpe's head jug from them. Just a skill he's got."

"How do you know this corpse is really the Tennessee Kid? Or that the jug of bone ain't just full of animal bones or such?"

"I . . . I just know."

"You're taking your partner's word for it, you mean."

"You have an impudent tongue in your head, son."

"I know I do. Sorry. But I can't help wondering how you *know* what you are showing is real. My pa always says that showmen are mostly storytellers, by which he means liars. No offense. It's why he ain't allowed me to go see the Outlaw Train. He says nobody should hand over money to see a bunch of fake corpses and doodads and such."

"Well, now that you've got that pass, you can come to the train without your father being out so much as a nickel. So I'll expect to see you there. Now, can we go in and find that whiskey?"

"Yeah. But I'll warn you, there ain't much left in the bottle, as I recall it."

"A little is better than none. Come on, son."

They walked to the house of Ben Keely, and Jakey Wills turned the key in the lock. No more than a minute later, Gypsy Nicholas Anubis was seated in the corner of Keely's front room with a glass of whiskey in hand, enjoying it along with the prospect of finishing off what still remained in the bottle.

Jakey, a little nervous because he'd let a stranger, without permission, into the home of a man who had trusted him, fidgeted in his seat a few minutes while Anubis drank, then began pacing around the small living room, looking at the handful of books on Ben Keely's shelves.

"Here's one called *Well-Known Bad Men of the Frontier*," he announced as he pulled it down from the shelf. "Let me see here. . . ." Jakey thumbed through it, found the index, and scanned. "Yep. There's something here about the Harpes. 'Big and Little Harpe,' it says. Which one's skull bone do you have? I forgot."

"Big Harpe. He got killed and beheaded in Kentucky. His brother died later. Somewhere down in the lower Mississippi River country, I think." Anubis took another sip of whiskey and smacked his lips. "Not bad whiskey for a backwater lawman to have on his shelf. I'm going to finish off this bottle, son, and thank you for it."

"Well, you're welcome, because I don't figure Ben is coming back. He'd have come by now if he was going to."

"So how's your town fixed for law, with your marshal gone?"

"We got a substitute. One of Ben's deputies, name of Luke Cable. Does a right fair job, but lately he's had some trouble. The county sheriff got gunned down in one of the saloons, and after they locked up the shooter, the man got the jump on one of the jailers when nobody else was there, and killed him right through the bars. Snapped his neck clean as a hangman, with his hands. Know who it was?"

"How would I know your local jailers, son?"

"I'm talking about the prisoner, not the jailer. It was one of the Nolan brothers. Scar Nolan. Or that's what everybody believes. He claimed some other name. But that's what you'd expect a wanted outlaw like Nolan to do, claim a false name."

"You're telling me Scar Nolan is locked up in your local jail?"

"No. He broke out. He took the key off the jailer's corpse and let himself out. Got a horse and fled. The marshal has a posse out looking for him right now."

Anubis rubbed his chin thoughtfully while thunder rumbled through the clouded sky outside. "Intriguing, boy. Absolutely intriguing! And a little worrisome."

"Why worrisome?"

"I'd as soon not say. Suffice it to say he might have cause to be a bit unhappy with me and my associate. I have to wonder if he followed us here. I've had a feeling somebody's been following us for a while now."

"None of my business, I reckon, but why would Scar Nolan have something against two showmen?"

"Because we got something on the train that he most likely wouldn't like us having."

The man drank some more and the boy continued to restlessly pace about. As Anubis poured the last of Ben Keely's whiskey into his glass, he eyed Jakey with one brow slightly raised. "Son, let me ask you a question. Have you heard any talk about a woman, kind of a fortune-teller or something, who is in your town right now?"

"There is a woman who's held a meeting, talking to the dead kin of folks who came to it."

"Hmm. What's her name?"

"House, or Hoss, or something like that."

"Heard any talk about her?"

"Joe Farner, who lives over yonder way a few miles, rode by yesterday and said something about her. Said she's a real pretty woman."

"Did he say she was a fallen woman? A whore?"

"No. But we didn't talk for long. He was just riding through to visit some of his people further to the west."

"We've run across that same woman before, Percival and me, while we travel. And she is indeed a fallen woman. Makes part of her money that way, part by pretending to get messages from the dead. And there's a chance she's not really named Haus. There's a good chance her real name is Kate Bender. You've heard of her, I suppose?"

"I've heard of the Bender family who had that inn where they killed folks."

"That's who I'm talking about."

"Is it really her?"

"Don't know. But if it is, I wish she'd visit the Outlaw Train and fall over dead while she was there. She'd be quite the display, that particular woman's corpse."

Jakey had to ponder how strange a man this was he'd allowed into Ben Keely's house. "How would you keep her corpse from going bad on you?"

"Same way I've preserved the others, like Tennessee out there. That's my trained skill, son, preserving the dead. It's what I know how to do, better than anybody else in this nation. This woman Haus talks to the dead. Me, I preserve them."

"But even an undertaker can't make a corpse last for good."

"Not if he hasn't been trained in certain secret old arts that make it possible. Me, I've been trained. I've been taught the old arts. In my field, son, I'm a famous man, in one small circle. No other like me. No other at all, not since my teacher passed on. No one else alive knows what I know about preserving the dead."

"So who will know when you're gone?"

"What do you mean, gone?"

"Well . . . nobody lives forever."

"I'm not an old man yet."

"No . . . but nobody lives forever."

"Well, I . . . I don't know. I haven't given it a thought."

"You ought to teach somebody else."

Anubis rubbed his hand across his chin and looked distressed. After a few moments he said, "No. I can't do that."

"Why not?"

"Because then I wouldn't be the only one. It's good, you see, to be the only one. It's all I've got . . . being the only one."

CHAPTER FIFTEEN

Jimmy Wills, seated behind the desk of the Gable House Hotel, looked up quickly when he realized he had a customer. He'd been absorbed in a dime novel, something he counted on to help him pass what promised to be a boring day. Mr. Gable had moved him off night duty, a positive change, in Jimmy's view, but he'd been surprised to find that the only difference now was that daytime rather than night had become an endless drudgery.

Jimmy slipped the novel onto a shelf under the desk and stood to welcome the newcomer. The raven-haired man was dressed like a typical traveler, but Jimmy noticed his clothing, though of seemingly high quality, was threadbare and worn. Old. His hat bore the dark stains of much wear and handling. This man was accustomed to travel, and was no man of means.

What intrigued him about the man, though, were his eyes. They were quite large and extraordinarily blue, but not the kind of pale, dog's-eye blue that made some people striking, but a deep, almost lavender hue, made more obvious in contrast to his pallid complexion. The thought that crossed Jimmy's mind as he looked at the stranger was that this man came from some exotic, and definitely European, ancestry.

"Good day, sir," Jimmy said brightly. "Welcome to the Gable House."

"Thank you," the man replied in an accent that sounded familiar to Jimmy, though he couldn't remember just where he'd heard another like it. As the man continued to speak, though, Jimmy made the connection. Katrina Haus. That's who he talked like. "I'm a traveler in need of a room, young man. Have you anything available?"

"We do, sir," Jimmy said. "Your choice of any of four rooms at the moment."

"All of equal quality?"

"They are. All with a good bed, extra pillows, extra quilts in the trunk at the foot of the bed—though you won't need those in this warm weather—and cherrywood wardrobes with a dozen hangers each. There's a basin on a washstand, and every morning our guests find a pitcher of heated water outside their door by eight o'clock, with a clean towel and washcloth. We also offer a free razor-sharpening service for our guests in conjunction with the general hardware store down the street. And discounted meals for our guests in the Almanac Café over on Emporium Street."

"Emporium Street . . . named for the Montague's Emporium that is making your town so famous?"

"It is. Though I don't know that our town is 'famous,' exactly."

"Well, I can tell you that word about that remarkable establishment has spread far and wide. The nearest store to compare to Montague's Emporium, I've been told, is in Chicago, far from here."

"It is a big place, no doubt about it. I wasn't sure the emporium would survive here, with the size of our population, but it draws customers from miles away. Many people travel to Wiles just to visit the place. It's been good for this town, sir."

"The town of Wiles owes a great deal to Mr. Montague."

"How long do you anticipate staying with us, Mr. . . ."

"Baum. Fredrick Baum. Two nights at least. Perhaps more if the ground here proves fertile. I speak metaphorically in that regard."

He might as well have been speaking Greek as far as Jimmy Wills was concerned. Jimmy had no notion what a word such as "metaphorically" meant. The "fertile ground" reference made him assume that Baum was in some way involved in agriculture.

"If you need to extend your stay, that will be no problem. We give preference to lodgers already in place. Now, if you wish to sign in . . ."

Jimmy turned the ledger around to allow Baum to put his name on the first open line. While signing, Baum scanned previous names. He lifted a forefinger and touched the name of Katrina Haus higher on the register page.

"You know her?" Jimmy asked.

"Years ago, back in Pennsylvania, from where I come, I knew a girl by that name, while both of us were children. A beautiful girl . . . the first I ever took notice of, if you understand me."

"The Katrina Haus who is staying here is a very beautiful woman," Jimmy said. "The most beautiful I've seen."

"I'll keep an eye peeled, then. Doubtful it would be the same person, though."

"Probably not." Jimmy fished a ringed key off the pegboard behind him. "May I help you get your bags upstairs?"

"I have only what I'm already carrying," Baum replied. "I'll manage alone. But thank you." He hefted his things and stepped toward the stair. "Would it be improper for me to ask what room Miss Haus is staying in?"

"She's right down the hall from the room I just put you in, sir," Jimmy replied. "Two doors, same side of the corridor as you."

"Thank you, sir. I look forward to my stay in your hotel."

"Glad to have you with us, Mr. Baum."

Baum started again toward the stairs, then stopped. "Oh, young man," he said, "I take it you are a reader. I saw you reading a book when I came in."

"Helps to pass the time."

"Let me give you something you might enjoy, then." He set down his bags, opened one of them, and from it produced something that at first Jimmy thought was another dime novel, or perhaps an almanac. Baum laid it on the desk in front of Jimmy.

SPRING-HEELED JACK'S ARGUS OF MYSTERY, the illustrated cover read. Then a smaller line of ornamental type beneath: *A Compendium of the Strange, Spiritual, and Supernatural from across the United States of America.*

The illustration, an etching similar in style to what Jimmy had seen in such publications as *Harper's* and *Leslie's Illustrated*, showed a woman on the street of some city, cowering by night from an apparition that loomed out of a dark alley, leaning over her like a giant made of smoke. Beneath the image were the words Ghosts of the Philadelphia Backstreets, a Study by F.A.B.

"That's me, 'F.A.B.,'" Baum said. "Frederick Allen Baum."

Jimmy picked up the paper-bound volume and studied the picture closely. "You print this thing?" he asked.

"No, but I write for it. And I work closely with the illustrators who provide the excellent art such as you see on that cover."

"So this thing is about ghosts and such?"

"It is a periodical journal that explores those mysteries that confront us in this world, particularly when it intersects with worlds beyond. Do you understand me?"

"I ain't sure."

"Then let me put it this way: it's about 'ghosts and such.' The 'and such' part being a broad category indeed."

"I don't know of ghosts in Wiles, mister."

"Oh, there may be some. There are often ghosts in places where violent death has occurred. And small Western towns such as this one are known as sites of violent death."

"Not Wiles. We're known for nothing much happening." He paused. "Except . . . our county sheriff just got killed by a famous outlaw. Scar Nolan. Shot him dead. Marshal's posse is still out looking for him, far as I know."

"Any evidence of ghostly activity where your sheriff died?"

"He ain't even buried yet, mister. I figure a ghost would at least wait for the burying before he stirred himself."

"Well . . . no matter. I didn't come to this town on the hope of stumbling upon some random ghost tale."

"Why, then?" By the standards of the Kansas frontier, this was an intrusive question, and Jimmy knew it, but he was too curious not to ask.

"I'm on . . . a *trail*. The trail of a particular story. This is the place, I think, where I will find it."

"Well, good luck to you in that, sir. Most times there's nothing in this town with the least bit of excitement to it."

"Sometimes a town has its own excitement, and sometimes excitement comes to it."

"Let me know if you find any problem with your room, Mr. Baum."

"Thank you, young man."

Baum hefted his things and started toward the stairs again. But Jimmy said, "Sir, I told you I knew of no ghosts in Wiles. And that's true, except that there was a meeting here in the last little bit where folks gathered and talked to their dead kin. It was Miss Haus who led it."

"Really? She is a medium?"

"She says she can talk to spirits of the departed. I saw her doing it . . . it was my job to collect the admission money at the door."

"Did she succeed at her task?"

"She seemed like she did. She told a lot of folks a lot of things they seemed to want to hear. About their dead children being in heaven and all. So I guess she must have gotten through to the spirits."

"There are ways, really quite simple ones, by which such things can be faked. Did you see manifestations? Mists? Smokes? Plasmas? Audible voices coming from nowhere?"

"Nothing like that, no."

"I see." Baum pursed his lips and knit his brows. "I see."

He headed up the stairs, carrying whatever thoughts he had with him in silence.

Jimmy, meanwhile, was glad the subject of Katrina Haus had come up. It reminded him that there was something he needed to give her. Something he'd found on the hotel desk when he arrived for his shift. He put his hand into a drawer and withdrew it.

It was an envelope, sealed with wax, with the name of Katrina Haus on the front of it. He had no idea who had left it.

Jimmy laid the envelope out near the ledger so he would be sure to see it when Katrina next came in. And as luck would have it, she walked into the lobby within the next five minutes, and headed toward the stairs. Baum was long gone by now, locked away up in his room.

"Ma'am," he said. She turned. He held up the envelope. "Someone left this for you."

She took the envelope and unsealed it on the spot. Pulling out a folding note card, she opened it and read quickly. Jimmy recognized the monogram on the outside of the card. It was one of the personalized note cards used by banker Howard Ashworth for his informal correspondence.

To Jimmy's surprise, Katrina brought the card over to him. Covering up much of the writing inside with her hand, she let him see a few words.

"Tell me, Jimmy," Katrina asked, "does this writing look like Mr. Ashworth's writing to you?"

He glanced at it and shook his head. "The impression it gives me, ma'am, is of a woman's hand."

"I thought the same." Katrina pulled the card back and frowned at it.

"What is your concern, ma'am?"

Katrina looked up at Jimmy. "I probably shouldn't . . . oh, what does it matter? I'm certain you know what I do. For my living, I mean. Other than my communications with the departed."

"I think I know what you're referring to, ma'am."

"Well, then you'll understand why I find it odd that the wife of a man with whom I've . . . done, well, 'business' would write a note requesting me to meet her husband in a private location, and sign her husband's name to it. That's what this note is. A request supposedly from Howard Ashworth to meet me in a dark lot near the emporium building. His name is signed, but I'm inclined to believe this was done by his wife."

"I don't think you should go, Miss Haus," Jimmy said. "Maybe she knows you were with him before. Maybe she's got bad designs. Or, maybe they just want to thank you for putting their dead son in touch with them at your presentation."

"Maybe so." She thought about it a few moments

and seemed to seize upon the idea. "I'm sure you are right, Jimmy. They simply want to thank me."

"Or maybe Mr. Ashworth has just got a womanish way of writing," Jimmy suggested.

"It's possible." Katrina laughed musically. "You have been a most helpful young man while I've been in this town," she said. "Before I depart here, I am thinking of, shall we say, *rewarding* you in a special way."

Jimmy tried to speak, but his voice had disappeared.

Katrina Haus laughed and went up the stairs to her room. There she looked again at the card bearing Howard Ashworth's monogram and signature, and marked in her mind the time and place of the requested meeting. It was this same day, the time not very far away.

She listened to a peal of thunder and regretted that the weather was turning bad. She would proceed nonetheless. Maybe the storm would come and go before she met Ashworth in that lot near the emporium.

CHAPTER SIXTEEN

Percival Raintree stood beside the railroad car that housed Gypsy Nick Anubis's rolling embalming chamber, and studied the sky. Dark and roiling clouds dominated, and the air felt thick with the threat of rain. The downpour would begin within fifteen minutes, Raintree estimated. As a traveling man usually separated from the natural world only by the thin walls of a railroad car, he'd become proficient at reading the weather, and was seldom wrong in his predictions.

Raintree looked at the shallow ruts left by Anubis's wagon when he'd left for Wiles earlier. Despite his partner's assurances, he was still uncertain it was a good idea to actually parade one of their main displays into the heart of town. Sure, it had worked elsewhere, enticing customers who might otherwise have never attended . . . but it was also a dangerous move, inviting uncomfortable questions from the local law. There were plenty of people out there who just couldn't shake off the notion that there had to be something wrong, morally, legally, or both, with displaying actual corpses or portions thereof. Never mind that there were museums all across the country and world displaying the mummified remains of ancient Egyptians, South American natives, American Indians, and others. Still, Raintree had been in his line of work long enough to conclude that sometimes it was best simply not to invite controversy in the first place. Come into a locale, hang a few advertising flyers around town, welcome the crowds, and move on quickly to the next stop.

The problem was, it simply wasn't working as well as it had at the beginning. Some years ago, when Perkins Ironwood, a part-Cherokee member of an acting troupe and habitual collector of oddities, had transformed himself into Percival Raintree, tattoo-eared showman of unspecified exotic origin and traveling displayer of outlaw relics and even dead outlaws themselves, the process had been simple and efficient. A simple covered wagon, highly decorated, had borne his collection of grim collectibles from town to town, and by help of his posted flyers and word-of-mouth, plenty of viewers had turned out night after night.

Raintree couldn't account for why it was no longer that way. The decline had started about a year and a half before, inexplicably, and had slowly but steadily worsened since then. Raintree wondered if the world simply was changing, and outlawry was losing its fascination in the public mind. Why would such a thing happen?

By the time of what, in his mind, he called "the change," he was working with Nicholas Anubis. Not that he held Anubis in any way accountable; in fact, Anubis's contributions to the show were equally as significant as their improved mode of travel. Gone was traveling by wagon. The wagon, sans its former cover, now was used merely for transport, and by Anubis whenever he made advertising forays into whatever town they happened to be nearby, as he had into the town of Wiles tonight.

Anubis. Raintree had mixed feelings about the man he had drawn in as a subordinate partner. Anubis had been a faithful and supportive associate, yet Raintree felt vaguely threatened by him. The hard truth was that Raintree's Outlaw Train operation, as it now was, needed Anubis much more than it needed Raintree himself.

It all had to do with Anubis's specialized skill and knowledge, knowledge he would not possess if not for Raintree. It was Raintree who had conceived the idea of moving beyond typical criminal relics such as guns, items of clothing, and so on, and adding actual bodies and body portions of dead outlaws, if such could be had.

There was an obvious problem, however, in the notion of hauling around corpses for an extended time: decomposition. And so Raintree had begun thinking, then researching, trying to find an answer. In that process he'd discovered he had a propensity for such prowling, information-gathering work; he'd discovered that, in Chicago, a very old man resided who purportedly possessed secrets that had enabled the ancient Egyptians to preserve the dead in a way that lasted for centuries. Raintree meticulously sought that man out, and after careful and delicate blandishments won his friendship. That process was made easier by the fact that the old man, Samuel Zuka, was near his own death and desirous of having his own remains preserved after death by the methods no one but he knew. Because a man could hardly mummify himself, Zuka at length agreed to Raintree's proposal to teach his art to an appropriate student, on condition that that student mummify and honor Zuka's corpse after he was gone.

Initially Raintree himself sought to be that pupil, but soon it became obvious he lacked the rudimentary embalming knowledge needed to understand adequately what Zuka had to teach. So Raintree had begun a search for an appropriate pupil, and found him in the person of David Akers. Akers was a Southerner who had learned the basics of embalming in the most rigorous classroom possible: Civil War battlefields. After the war, Akers had moved north to Illinois, seeking better opportunities. He was working as an embalmer's assistant in Chicago at the time Raintree located him.

Raintree followed Akers for days before a good opportunity to actually meet him arose. After making the man's acquaintance in an alley behind a Chicago saloon, he recruited Akers. It proved a good move. Akers was an apt pupil of Zuka's ancient arts, and by the time the old Egyptian finally passed away, the former undertaker's assistant had taken on his "Anubis" persona, was identifying himself as of Egyptian rather than Cherokee descent, and was thoroughly devoted to the life of a traveling showman.

The biggest challenge facing the "Outlaw Train," apart from maintaining an adequate supply of certain rare salts and drying agents used in the body preservation process, was, naturally, obtaining bodily relics of the criminal dead. Raintree proved himself capable in this regard, managing to purchase, from the family, the corpse of a lynched small-time criminal from Missouri named Fred Parks. "You want to pay for him, you got him," Parks's father had said. "The boy has brought naught but sorrow to his mother and me all his living years; maybe he can recompense for it a bit now that he's dead."

Under the hands of "Gypsy Nick Anubis," the rapidly declining corpse of Fred Parks was turned into a leathery, but decay-proof, display laid out on a slab that folded down from the interior back wall of the museum car like a prisoner's bunk in some dungeon. The imagination of Percival Raintree concocted for the insignificant criminal a fictional biography to rival that of the James brothers, and soon Fred Parks was being gaped at by hordes of small-towners and rural rubberneckers across the West.

The late Zuka himself, who had indirectly made the entire thing possible, soon went on display as well, fictionalized into an "Indian Mummy" of an ancient Choctaw chief who had died half a century before after a life of bloodthirsty carnage against the white race. Thus the skilled mummy-maker who had asked only that his remains be honored instead had them become a kind of insider's joke between Raintree and Anubis. He lay there in quiet indignity, across from Fred Parks, to be examined by those willing to part with a few cents for an afternoon or evening of unsophisticated and morbid entertainment.

Leaning back against the second railroad car that

was part of his little kingdom—Anubis's rolling mummy factory, an embalmer's laboratory on wheels—Raintree watched the clouds build and wondered if Anubis would find a shelter somewhere in town under which to keep the Tennessee Kid from getting soaked by rain. Raintree didn't really know whether a cursory dampening would hurt a corpse that was as dried up as a tin of saltpeter, but it just made good common sense, in his mind, to keep such a thing dry.

Raindrops began to splatter the ground. Raintree headed for the freestanding little flight of stairs between the two sidetracked railroad cars. At the platform, he cut left into the museum car, the only one of the two cars open to the public. The other car, a converted boxcar, though labeled Traveling Cabinet of Infamous Preservations, was a work location, not a show car for public touring. It also doubled as sleeping quarters for Raintree and Anubis, though Raintree often opted to sleep under the stars, or under the wagon, to avoid the smells of the salts and other chemicals Anubis used in embalming. Anubis, unlike Raintree, didn't seem to mind them.

Restless and unhappy, Raintree looked around the cluttered railroad car. Over months of effort, he and Anubis had filled the mobile museum with a visually impressive array of displays, quite varied but all having the common factor of connection with criminality. Weapons dominated: pistols, rifles, shotguns, knives, even a couple of sabers. Mounted on a plaque were three flattened, misshapen bullets that had been dug from the body of a bank clerk shot down during a robbery.

There were, of course, photographs and journalistic sketches, newspaper accounts preserved behind glass, and several images of slain outlaws propped up in slanted coffins, surrounded by lawmen and townsfolk who looked every bit as stiff as the dead. There was a Bible with a bullet hole penetrating half its depth, the questionable story being that it had saved the life of a camp meeting preacher from Texas whose exhortations had roused the ire of an outlaw in the crowd named Stanley Horton. Horton supposedly had stood and fired his pistol from the crowd. The preacher, seeing him rise and draw, had held up his Bible as a shield, and the bullet had struck at an angle, lodging somewhere in the book of Nahum. Raintree had examined the Bible, naturally, and read the verse that the bullet had nudged up against. That part had worked out well, from the perspective of a showman; the verse read "The Lord is good, a strong hold in the day of trouble; and he knoweth them that trust in him."

On the signboard that went with the displayed "bullet Bible," Raintree had written out the story, embellishing it slightly by declaring that the miraculously rescued-from-death preacher had gone on to preach an entire sermon from that verse while lawmen at the camp meeting wrestled away the shootist and "restored peace amidst the congregation of the righteous."

Raintree moved slowly through his exhibit, looking at each item closely despite his familiarity with them. He was looking at one particularly gruesome item, a raggedly severed hand, minus two fingers, still attached to a portion of a forearm, when a noise behind him, back at the door, made him turn.

A thirtyish man, a little rumpled and dirty at the moment, clothes drooping as if he'd been in the rain a good deal that day, opened the door and stepped inside. Raintree turned and faced him, and noted the badge on his vest.

"Hello, sir," Raintree said, smiling fulsomely. "Welcome to the Outlaw Train. But I'm sorry to tell you the exhibits are closed tonight."

"Closed? How can you make money if you don't open your exhibit?"

"Bad weather today, sir," Raintree replied. "I've been at this long enough to know that people simply won't come out for entertainment when the weather is unstable. And I've traveled this part of the country enough to know that this weather, this time of year, can turn to something far worse. My name is Raintree, by the way. Percival Raintree."

The other came forward, hand extended. "Luke Cable. Marshal of the town of Wiles, which lies over that direction." He pointed vaguely.

"Marshal."

"Well . . . acting marshal, technically speaking. The appointed full marshal left the area sometime back and hasn't returned." He paused, remembering the figure seen earlier on the ridge. "Or if he has, he hasn't showed himself."

"Interesting," Raintree replied. There was much more he could have said about the missing marshal of Wiles, Kansas, but certainly he would not. "I am familiar with Wiles," he went on, deflecting the line of the conversation a little. "In fact, my business associate is there this evening, carrying one of our display items on a wagon. A form of advertising to draw out crowds to see the rest of the show."

"Interesting concept you've got here," Luke said. "But I have to tell you, I've heard little talk of it in town. Have you been seeing good turnout?"

Raintree sighed and his smile went sad. "Not here, no, just to be fully truthful. I can't account for it. Normally we get a better response." It wasn't entirely true; public interest had been declining well before the Outlaw Train came to Wiles.

Luke said, "There's been some competition in Wiles from a woman claiming to be able to communicate with the dead. Maybe she's cut into your business."

"Maybe so, sir."

Luke looked around, then said, "I know you are not open for business, but since I'm here, might I receive a tour? I'll gladly pay your admission price."

"No need for admission, sir. In that you are a peace officer, I am glad to provide you a tour free of charge."

"Very obliging of you, sir. And this gives me a chance to give you a word of warning I believe you are due."

"Beg your pardon? What have I done to create any need for warning?"

Luke took a slow breath. "Do you have here any relics related to a family named Nolan? I'm speaking of the outlaw Nolan brothers who have become rather infamous."

Raintree lifted his brows high. "The famous Nolan Brothers Gang, eh?" He paused, weighing something.

"Yes, yes. We do indeed have something here re-lated to the Nolans. A part of one of them, in fact."

"Part of?"

"You know how Billy Nolan died, Marshal?"

"An accident involving blowing up a safe, I think."

"That's right. He lost part of his arm, and what remained of the hand on that arm was lacking some fingers."

"Sounds gruesome."

"Would you like to see for yourself?" Raintree smiled and waved toward the display he'd been ex-amining when Luke entered.

Luke looked it over and whistled softly. "How did you get *that*?"

"I have a talent for finding and for acquiring," Raintree replied. "At the outset of my work, I had the support of a wealthy benefactor in St. Louis, a man obsessed with the collection of criminal relics. He provided me a rich supply of funds with which to obtain the curiosities he wanted. So initially I was a collector for a purely private museum collection, kept in his home and never open to the public. When at length he died, I was operating my traveling cabi-net of curiosities on a small scale, out of a wagon. When I learned of my benefactor's passing, I con-tacted his son with my condolences, and was sur-prised with the gift of many of the best relics I had collected for him. The son had no interest in his late father's 'morbidities,' as he termed them. With an additional inheritance of cash from my late friend, I was able to outfit this railroad car and present my exhibitions on a far grander scale. When I added my partner Mr. Anubis, I obtained a second railcar and outfitted it for his own special work, which makes much of what you see here possible. Meanwhile, I continually procure relics. When I learn of one, I track it down and find a way to obtain it."

"Legal ways?"

Raintree gaped a moment, then grinned. "I suppose I cannot take offense at that question. You are, after all, a lawman. To answer you, yes, my means are legal. I display criminals, Marshal, but I am not one myself. Consider me a seller, not a buyer. Unless what I'm buying is something that can become part of my Outlaw Train."

Luke was still staring at the ugly piece of severed meat that once had been the right arm of one of Scar Nolan's younger brothers. "What are you thinking about, Marshal?" Raintree asked.

"I'm thinking about a couple of things. One is the warning I need to give you."

"Please. I'm listening."

Luke looked the tattooed showman in the eye. "I spent today leading a posse, looking for an escapee from my own jail. We looked all day with no luck. Know who that prisoner was?"

"I'll take a guess: Kate Bender."

It was Luke's turn to gape. "Kate Bender? Why would you guess *that* name?"

"My associate, Mr. Anubis, stumbled across some story regarding the woman in your town communicating with spirits. There are those who believe she is actually the infamous Miss Bender, it would seem."

"I've heard the same speculation, which to my knowledge is all it is. Speculation. The escapee we chased today was not her. It was Scar Nolan."

"You are sure?"

"I can't prove it. He claims the name of Wesson. But I'm confident he is Scar Nolan. And I doubt I need to say what my concern is regarding what his attitude might be toward your Outlaw Train here."

"He might be resentful regarding the display of his brother's lost arm and hand," Raintree said.

"Yes. And believe me, you don't want such a one as Scar Nolan angry with you. I saw what he did to my jailer. Killed him bare-handed through the bars of his cell."

"I'll be quite cautious, Marshal, and thank you for the warning."

Luke squinted at the ruin of an arm. "How do you keep it from decaying?" he asked.

"Therein lies the contribution of Mr. Anubis. He possesses certain ancient skills he applies to keep flesh from decaying beyond the most superficial degradation."

Interesting, Luke thought, suddenly pondering the mysterious mummified leg Charlie Bays's son had found beside the railroad tracks. It might be worthwhile to have a conversation with this Anubis fellow.

Luke noted a vacant spot in the crowded display. "What's supposed to be there?" he asked.

"That's where the preserved corpse of the late Tennessee Kid usually is seated," Raintree replied. "He is one of our best displays, a favorite of the public. One of our more recent additions, too."

"Where is he now?"

"He is in your town, on a wagon seat, being paraded about by Mr. Anubis in hope of drawing visitors to our train," Raintree replied. "Tennessee's head, of course, is covered, given that the poor fellow died from a shotgun blast to the face. That's not something we're willing to show the public. Our goal is to entertain, not to sicken."

"That blown-off arm there comes close enough to sickening, as far as I'm concerned," Luke said, nodding at the ugly display. "There's another thing you've got I'm interested in: the thing on the sign outside. The jar with the crumbled-up skull of Micajah Harpe."

Raintree's mind worked fast. He knew what was probably prompting the marshal's interest in that particular item, and it was important to handle the situation carefully.

"I know why you ask. You ask because the jar was formerly in possession of a Kentucky family named Keely," Raintree ventured. "Am I right? And that same Keely family is the family of your own missing town marshal."

"Exactly. So naturally I have to wonder how you came into possession of that item, and if it has anything to do with the fact that Ben Keely has not returned to Kansas."

"Marshal, I obtained that jar . . . you can see it over there . . . directly from Ben Keely himself. I had tracked the lore of the Harpes for some time and had learned the name of the family into whose hands the jar had passed, and where they could be found. I paid a visit to Kentucky and was fortunate enough to locate Marshal Keely in a backwoods restaurant. We talked and he agreed to sell me the jar of bone."

"Did he say anything about returning to Kansas? Because he has not done that."

"Our discussion didn't run in that direction. We shook hands, passed the jar, parted, and that was the end of the story. I am surprised to learn he has not come back here."

"Well, maybe he has. I think I saw him today."

Raintree seemed to freeze. "Saw Marshal Keely?"

"Yes. From a distance, admittedly, but it appeared to be him. And I'm not the only one who saw him today, or for that matter, earlier. My own jailer, for one, saw a rider he swears was Ben, near the jailhouse."

"I . . . I don't think . . . I . . ."

"What's wrong, Mr. Raintree? Why do you seem so surprised? If you parted from Ben Keely in Kentucky, maybe he just decided it was time to return."

"Uh . . . yes. Yes. You are right, of course."

"Is there something you're not telling me, Mr. Raintree? You seem shocked at the notion of Ben Keely being back in Kansas."

"No, no, sir. I've told you all I know."

"Truth is, Mr. Raintree, I'm surprised Ben would sell that Harpe jar to you. When he was leaving Wiles he talked about how much he wanted to bring that back with him, to remember his father by. It was an important item to his father, it seems."

"All I can tell you is that he did sell it to me, Marshal. Every man has his price. Beyond that, I know nothing of what he did or whether he has come back here, or sprouted wings and flown off to the moon."

"Why are you angry, sir?"

"I'm . . . I'm not. I apologize. Tense days, these, with business being slack."

Luke looked around a few moments more, pausing longest at the Harpe jar, though there was little there to look at. "Thank you for showing me around, Mr. Raintree. And good luck with your train here, and in the future. And do keep a lookout for anybody coming around who could be Scar Nolan. I don't know he'd cause you a problem, but I got a feeling he might."

"Thank you, Marshal. Good evening to you."

"Maybe I'll see your partner when I get back to town."

"Maybe so. He'll be easy to spot. He'll be the one on a wagon with a dead outlaw beside him."

Luke began to leave, but turned suddenly. "One more thing, Mr. Raintree. There was a leg found very recently beside the railroad tracks on the far side of Wiles. A cut-off leg."

"Interesting. Terrible reality of railroads, how sometimes people are struck and mangled."

"This leg had been surgically removed. And it was preserved. And I mean well preserved. Like that severed arm you got displayed there. And the leg was found right about the same time your Outlaw Train here would have been rolling through these parts on its way to this particular sidetrack."

"Marshal, I know nothing about any such thing." Raintree paused and grinned. "It's good that our friend the Tennessee Kid isn't here to listen to us. He might want to borrow that leg to replace his own."

Luke gave an obligatory chuckle and again started to leave. But again he paused and turned.

"Mr. Raintree, just what kind of trousers are on the corpse of the Tennessee Kid?"

"I . . . I don't recall. I've never thought to pay attention. Why?"

Luke shrugged. "No reason. Just asking."

He left.

Luke had moved only twenty feet away from the train when it hit him. He couldn't have said what "it" was, though, because it came so fast and without warning. A sense of being physically jolted from head to toe, a flashing pain and a brilliant flash of light, and suddenly he was on the ground, blacking out before he even had time to finish the thought: *I've just been struck by lightning.*

But hadn't been that it. What had struck him was the butt of a Henry rifle, one stolen out of the town of Wiles marshal's office by the man now bearing it: Scar Nolan. Nolan had crept out from behind the Outlaw Train as Luke left, and had sneaked silently behind the lawman as he led his horse away, getting ready to mount and finally return to town as the rest of his posse had already done.

Nolan looked down at Luke Cable's senseless form and grinned. "Looks like you found me, Marshal," he said softly. "And you thought I was gone for good. Sorry I had to disappoint you." Nolan chuckled. "I got some advice for you, lawman. You need to get yourself some better posse members, and better jailers. It was easy as could be, breaking that stupid fellow's neck back in your jailhouse. And just as easy to give your posse the slip. Hell, Marshal, I watched you boys most of the day, watched you running around like no-headed chickens, biggest pack of fools I ever run across! You might want to find you another line of work, Mr. Marshal. I don't think you're cut out for this one."

Luke Cable, who could hear none of it, groaned unconsciously and earned himself another clout to the head for it. Then Scar Nolan dragged him away to a nearby small stand of trees, and set Luke up against one of them. He pulled the marshal's arms back and tied his wrists together on the opposite side of the tree, using a length of rope taken from Luke's own saddlebag. He tied off Luke's horse to a bush.

Then Scar Nolan glanced up at the murky sky, watched a bolt of lightning fire down to some point on the mostly flat horizon, and shook his head.

"Lordy, Marshal, for your sake I hope none of that lightning hits this here tree," he said. Then, laughing to himself, he headed back toward the display car of the Outlaw Train.

It was time to settle a small point of Nolan family honor.

Percival Raintree was occupied with dusting off a neglected area of the exhibit when Scar Nolan opened the door and entered the museum car.

"Did you forget something, Marshal?" Raintree asked before he looked to see that the intruder was not his previous visitor. He froze, breathless, as the big man with the scarred face walked in and stared coldly at him.

"I'm no marshal, not by a long shot," Nolan said. "My name is Nolan, though lately I've gone by the name of Wesson just to make it a little easier to get by without trouble. But I've got to tell you, sir, that trouble has now come to you and your little curiosity train here."

Imprudent though it was to do it, Raintree couldn't restrain himself from glancing at the ugly display showing the severed hand and arm portion from Billy Nolan, one of Scar's brothers. Nolan's eyes followed Raintree's, and his gaze locked on the preserved and ragged piece of flesh and bone.

"So it's true, what I've heard," Nolan said. "You truly are using the flesh of my own kin to make yourself money off their misfortune."

"You are Scar Nolan, sir?" Raintree said.

"I am. And I've come to set right the wrong you've done to my family."

"All I've done, sir, is to display items of interest to the public. It is a legitimate business that meets a demand of the people, and no dishonor is intended."

"Well, I don't like it, my poor brother's hand being showed off like that, and I know my dear mother and his wouldn't have liked it. I'll have you take that down now, sir, and turn it over to me."

Raintree, though, had other ideas, though he would have to move quickly if he was to carry them out. Scar Nolan was a criminal, a murderer, arguably the worst of the Nolan brothers . . . and having the preserved corpse of such a man would be a far greater coup than anything he had achieved so far.

"Very well, sir," Raintree said, pulling a key from his pocket and moving toward the display case containing the blown-off, damaged hand. But as he turned to the side, he slipped the key back into his pocket, seized the pitchfork that had taken the life of gunfighter Curly Drake, and without hesitation or allowance of any time for Scar Nolan to see what was coming, jammed the tines of the implement into Nolan's chest. He drove in hard, aiming for the area of the heart.

Nolan squeaked and groaned and staggered back, eyes bulging in pain and horror, staring at his killer in utter surprise. Raintree shoved the pitchfork again, and just as he went down to the floor of the railroad car, Nolan pulled a pistol from his belt and used the final three seconds of his waning life to shoot Percival Raintree through the forehead, splattered blood and brain across the colorful displays of the Outlaw Train.

Both men died at almost the same moment, neither living long enough to hear the incredibly loud roaring noise that suddenly surrounded the railroad cars.

The twister, massive, black, and powerful, lifted the Outlaw Train from the side track, pitched it about in the air like a bad child abusing his toy, and smashed it back to the earth, breaking it open like an eggshell and dumping the relics of dead outlaws all about on the ground and sending them flying like autumn leaves through the air.

Chapter Seventeen

Dewitt Stamps laid his open Bible flat on the desk-top and rubbed his tired eyes. "Lord, help me this evening," he murmured softly, but aloud. "I'm drawn toward sin this evening. Help me, Lord, to stay strong."

The window above the desk, which faced the street, rattled in a burst of wind, startling the jailer. Dewitt jumped and sucked in his breath sharply, and listened in alarm as the wind continued to shake the pane. It rose from a steady humming to nearly a howl.

Dewitt stood and shuddered, partly from a cool wind that had found its way in around the edges of the loose pane, partly because of an inner nervousness that made him cold.

"Lord, Luke, when you coming back?" he asked the empty room. "Your posse came back two hours ago. So where are you?"

He went out onto the jail porch to make a better assessment of just how strong the wind was likely to grow. If a damaging storm, or worse, struck the town, those in the marshal's office would have many duties and public expectations thrown at them . . . and Dewitt wasn't sure he was up to that kind of task. Where was Luke? Why had he not come back?

"Lord, I need help," he said. "This is more of a task than I can bear. Send me help, Lord. Send Luke home."

Movement on the street made him turn his head, and he saw a rider coming his way. Luke? He looked closely and saw that, no, it was not Luke . . . but it hardly mattered. Dewitt's heart raced with happiness to see what appeared to be an answer to his prayer appearing right before him.

He stepped down from the porch and walked toward the rider with a big smile on his face. "Ben, is that you? Is that really you? Have you come back at last? Ben! It's me, Dewitt! I'm working as a jailer now, thanks to Luke! Working right in your old office!"

The rider said nothing, but plodded closer. The impression that this was Ben Keely continued with Dewitt, but when the horse, which certainly looked like Ben's horse that Dewitt had rubbed down many times back in his days as a stable worker, made its final step and was gently reined to a halt, he suddenly wasn't so sure. Ben Keely was a man of small frame, certainly, but this individual struck him as even thinner. And when the dismounted rider stepped up onto the porch and looked Dewitt in the face, Dewitt was stricken with puzzlement and astonishment.

The face was remarkably like that of Ben, and the posture and general aura . . . but what Dewitt had taken to be a dust of whiskers on the cheeks and chin proved now to be a mere coating of grime.

And the eyes . . . they were like Ben's in a way, but more richly lashed . . . feminine.

"Hello, Mr. Cable," the newcomer said, and Dewitt might have choked in surprise. This was not Ben Keely, not by a far stretch.

This was a woman.

"I'm . . . I'm not Mr. Cable," he said, voice faltering. "Mr. Cable is the marshal . . . well, the fill-in marshal. I'm just a jailer. My name is Dewitt Stamps."

The woman reached up and took off her hat. There was no sudden spill of hair . . . this woman's hair was chopped short, extending no farther than the lobes of her ears.

She put out her hand toward Dewitt. "I'm pleased to meet you, Mr. Stamps. My name is Bess Keely. Marshal Ben Keely is my brother, my twin, in fact, and I came to town hoping I would find him."

"Well . . . come in, Miz Keely. Come in!"

Back inside the jail office, Dewitt did his best to play both insightful questioner and gracious host. He offered to build a fire in order to brew coffee for his visitor, but Bess declined.

"How did you know to ask for Luke Cable?" Dewitt queried.

"My brother was with me in Kentucky a while back," Bess said. "He told us he'd left his deputy, Luke Cable, in charge of the office in his absence. I remembered the name, and that's who I expected to find here. I'm sorry, Mr. Stamps, but I don't think Ben mentioned your name."

"That's because it was Luke who hired me, after Ben had already left and been gone a while," Dewitt said. "Ben don't know I work in this office now."

Bess looked forlornly at the toes of her own boots, thrust out before her. She was slumped in her chair, looking anything but ladylike in dress, attitude, and posture. Dewitt felt no surprise at all when she reached into a pocket and pulled out a cigar. She looked like the kind of female who would smoke a cigar. He lit it for her.

"I'm worried, Dewitt," she said, puffing. "Worried that something has happened to my brother."

"Everybody here's been worrying the same thing," Dewitt said. "It don't seem like Ben to keep himself away like he has."

"I fear he never left Kentucky, Dewitt. May I call you Dewitt?"

"'Course you can, ma'am."

"Call me Bess. 'Ma'am' ain't something I'm used to."

Dewitt was awash with curiosity about this strange woman. Why did she dress as she did? Why did she have such a masculine look and manner? Dewitt had heard Ben, in the past, talk about how he and his sister were not close, and how she was "odd" in some unspecified manner that created division within the family. Dewitt was beginning to suspect he was seeing some of that oddness right now.

"If Ben didn't leave Kentucky, why did you travel so far looking for him?" Dewitt asked. "Wouldn't you have seen him still there?"

"What I should have said was, I fear he might not have left Kentucky *alive*."

"Oh no. What are you thinking?"

"I talked with a man back home, a fellow named Bug Otis, old family friend, who had a meal with Ben right before Ben was going to the station to leave on the train heading to Kansas. There was a stranger who came and talked to the two of them, but mostly to Ben, trying to get Ben to sell him something that our family has owned for years, and that Ben had just gotten as an inheritance from our father. A jar, with the crumbled skull bone of a famous outlaw in it."

"I've heard talk about that. The Harpe's head jar, I think it was called."

"That's it. Well, Bug said that Ben refused to sell it to this man, which don't surprise me at all. He was proud to have inherited it, and I don't think he would sell it. But anyway, Ben never showed up to get on the train. And his horse was found roaming on a back road some ways from Mutton Smith's restaurant, which was where he and Bug had ate that meal together."

Dewitt puzzled over it a moment, then said, "Oh no, you don't think that other fellow followed Ben out and, and . . . and killed him to get that Harpe jar, do you?"

"That's exactly what I fear, Dewitt. Exactly. Especially when I found out from the railroad stationmaster that he'd gotten a wire or two from Wiles, Kansas, asking why Ben had never showed up back here. That's what made me decide I'd best come have a look myself."

"Why'd you take so long to show yourself once you got here? I caught a glance of you one time, off through some trees, and some others saw you from a distance and thought they were seeing Ben. Why didn't you come here to the office sooner than now? Seems like maybe . . ." Dewitt cut off speaking as a particularly loud clap of thunder shook the town. The glass in the jail office window rattled loudly.

Bess puffed her cigar until the coal was bright. "I didn't show myself right off because I wasn't sure how I was going to proceed with things," she said. "You see, the fellow who tried to buy that Harpe jar from Ben is a traveling showman, that's what Bug told me, and it ended up that fellow had come right here to Kansas himself, with his show train. And the truth is, I had it in mind to keep myself hid away, and track that showman for a while, and if I learned he'd killed my brother, by God, I was going to kill him in turn. Does it surprise you to hear me say that, Deputy?"

"I reckon not. But it still seems like you could have come and told Luke you was here."

"At that time I had it figured I was likely going to kill a man. You don't go announcing yourself to the local law when you're thinking about such a thing as that."

"I reckon you wouldn't. So why are you telling me now?"

"Because I've given up the notion of murder. I ain't got it in me to do that. Don't get me wrong . . . I care about my brother, even though me and him had a big falling-out and never had much to say to each other . . . but won't become a murderer over him. I ain't willing to pay that price."

"Well, you're thinking right. Murder is wrong, 'cording to God's word."

"You're a religious man, I take it?"

"I reckon you could say that. I used to be a bad man, drinking a lot, but this old sheep has found his way into the fold. And I want to stay there, and live right and holy . . . but lately it's been hard to not want to go back to my old ways. I want a drink mighty bad. Mighty bad." He shook his head. "But that would go against God's word."

Bess Keely smiled oddly. "I can show you, right in the Bible itself, where you might be wrong about that."

Dewitt gave her a wry look. "I got my doubts you can do that, Miz Keely."

"Call me Bess. And yes, I can do that. You got a Bible here?"

"Always keep one nearby." He reached over to the desk and produced his battered, much-handled copy, which he handed to Bess Keely.

Dewitt couldn't help judging her familiarity with the book by how deftly, or in her case, undeftly, she found what she was looking for. She flipped about randomly for more than a minute before finally narrowing in within a range of a few pages.

"Here it is," she said, smiling triumphantly and pointing at a particular verse. "I *knew* it was there! Want me to read it, or you want to read it yourself?"

"Go ahead and read it," he said.

Bess reached over and cranked up the wick of the oil lamp that illuminated the office, cleared her throat, and read: "Give strong drink unto him that is ready to perish, and wine unto those that be of heavy hearts." She looked up at Dewitt. "See? There's some Bible for you. If you are heavy-hearted, feeling ready to perish, go get yourself a drink. Bible tells you to."

Dewitt frowned and struggled for something to say, but could find nothing. Finally he said, "Let me see that," and grabbed the Bible from her. He scanned over the page, and she watched him move his lips as he read silently.

"I'll be!" he said, looking up at her. "You're right! I thought you'd just made that up." He looked back down at the page as his mind absorbed it. "Bess, I'm going to run down to the saloon and buy myself a drink. First one in four years."

"I'll go fetch it for you," she offered. "That way you can still see to the office here. Four years! Mister, you must be dry as dust."

"I am. You're mighty kind, ma'am. I mean, Bess."

"I do my best. I'll be back shortly."

When she was gone, Dewitt read the verse again and again. At last he set the Bible aside.

"Lord," he prayed out loud in the empty office, "I know I promised you I'd not drink liquor no more. But I reckon there must be no sin in it after all, if it's right there in your word. I'm heavy of heart, Lord. I'll only drink a little, Lord. Just a little. I promise."

CHAPTER EIGHTEEN

Wilton Brand was no drunkard, but on occasion he would tip a bottle if the mood struck him. That mood generally came at times he was lonely, or fresh from a visit with the wife who had divorced him three years earlier.

Neither of those situations applied this night, but Brand had been drinking all the same. Maybe it was the building stormy weather. He didn't know, and it didn't matter. He was drunk, and for the moment that suited him.

One thing didn't suit him, though: he was much in need of feminine company and feminine charms this night. And if he was lucky, he'd do better than old Belle Hart, who had been the most active soiled dove in the history of Wiles and a frequent paid conquest of Wilton Brand. Belle did the job well enough, but she, like Brand himself, was past her prime, and constituted overly explored territory. He was ready for new and fresher terrain.

As fate would have it, at that moment Brand's bleary eye was caught by a sweeping, graceful figure in pale blue, moving like a beautiful shadow down the boardwalk. Brand's breath failed him and he stopped in his tracks, watching Katrina Haus in lustful admiration.

His impulse was to hail her loudly and trot across to where she was, but some lingering social sensibility in his alcohol-pickled mind restrained him. In the brief time Haus had been in Wiles, people in the town had come to know not only who she was, but what she was . . . in *both* her lines of work. Discretion was demanded.

So without calling out to her, Brand started across the street, walking, not trotting. But just when he was close to her, she turned into a dark alleyway and was out of sight. Glancing around, Brand entered the same alley and hurried his pace in hope of catching up to the beautiful woman.

She had apparently moved quickly, because when he reached the back end of the alley and looked left and right, she was not to be seen. He stopped, slumped in disappointment, and muttered a few foul words softly.

"Oh well," he finally said, a little louder. "I guess my luck's bad tonight."

Just then he saw, farther down, a movement at ground level. A cat, probably, or maybe a squirrel or dog . . . but when he looked hard, squinting, he saw the movement again. It was the bottom edge of a woman's dress, extending out from around the corner of the rear of a building.

He chuckled, blessed his improving fortunes, and headed in that direction.

Oliver Wicks studied the sky and knew that what was coming was going to be worth seeing. He had an instinct for such things, and this, he was certain, would be no ordinary storm.

His eyes moved from the clouds to the familiar skyline of Wiles. If he was going to watch a storm, then he intended to do it from the best and highest vantage point he could find. Some danger from lightning, maybe, in doing that, but Oliver had defied lightning before, with no ill result.

He looked around a minute more, then with a curt nod made his decision. From the platform area of the Methodist church steeple, he could see the sky all around, and the far horizons, and still escape the worst of the rain.

Oliver trotted down the street, hoping no one would notice him, figure out what he was doing, and stop him. Grown people were funny like that, stopping boys from doing what they wanted to do, for no reason other than perceived danger.

Oliver reached the church without incident, and cast his eye on the strongly made trellis that ran up the east side of the white building. He went to it and began to climb, wincing against the new-falling raindrops that spattered his face.

Belle Hart had lived in Wiles for nearly a decade, and made her living in the same profession her late mother had followed in younger years. The old woman had hoped for something better for her daughter, but fate had not been kind. Belle, raised without a father by a woman who probably could not have identified the father anyway, had fallen into her mother's line of work naturally, perhaps inevitably, and had made only two attempts to find a more acceptable line of work, once as a seamstress, once as a librarian. Both efforts had failed. Back to the street Belle had gone.

She'd traveled around some. Wiles lived up to its reputation as one of the state's more sedate towns, the earthy lifestyles of Dodge, Abilene, and other cattle towns not being as prevalent. Even so, Belle usually found business enough in Wiles to maintain her living, but when times grew hard she'd never hesitated to move around to climes where sin was more welcomed. But in the end, it was always back to Wiles that she came. Back to home.

Standing at the rear of Hilbert's Alley, she was startled to feel a touch on her elbow. Wheeling, she came face-to-face with Wilton Brand, who looked back at her in a state of surprise equaling her own.

"Mr. Brand, sir!" she said, giving him a big smile. Belle had mastered the art of the insincere smile years ago.

"Belle . . . I'll be!"

"You were expecting someone else?" She chuckled in a friendly way as she said it.

"Well . . . I, uh . . ."

The smile faded as a realization came to Belle. Wilton Brand read it all in her face and knew he had to proceed diplomatically. A man didn't want to turn the town harlot against him. Women who knew a man's secret sins could do serious damage to that man's reputation, especially in a town that prided itself on its high moral tone.

"Cat got your tongue, Mr. Brand?" She lifted one

brow. "Or maybe it's that Dutch outsider who's run away with it!"

" 'Dutch outsider' . . . who do you mean, Belle?"

"You know who I mean, sir." Belle's mother had taught her to always maintain a certain formality with her clients, no matter how intimate she might be with them in the midst of conducting "business." "I'm talking about that Haus woman. The new, young whore who is here to run old whores like me out of business."

"I . . . I think I might have heard of her."

"Heard of her! The hell! She's the talk of this town, that strutting Jezebel is! Her name is everywhere, and God above knows she's all but ruined my business!" Belle paused, breathing oddly, and Brand was surprised to see her chin tremble. She was growing truly upset.

"Belle, are you all right?"

"You were looking for her, weren't you!"

"Of course not, Belle. I wouldn't know her if I saw her. You know it's you who I've always come to over the years. You and you alone."

She smiled again, with effort this time. She had to wonder how any man who practiced paid-for fornication could profess any kind of faithfulness. At the same time, though, she sensed that in Wilton Brand she might at least have a sympathetic listening ear, someone she could talk to about her increasing unhappiness with the current situation in this town.

"She's going to ruin me, Mr. Brand. Nobody wants the same old bag of bones when there's something young and fresh around."

"Pshaw! I came looking for you, didn't I?"

"Did you? Or was you really looking for *her*?"

Brand scratched at his jaw and paced around the end of the alley. "Well, Belle? You going to see to a needful man or not?"

"Lord have mercy, I've about lost the humor for it," Belle said.

"That won't go in your line of trade, woman!"

"I know it. Just talking honest, that's all." Belle paused and studied Brand closely. He was looking past her, toward the front end of the alley, staring hard. "What are you looking at, Mr. Brand?"

"There was a wagon just rolled past, out on the street. Two men in the seat. One of them looked to be . . . I swear . . . he had a sign held in front of him, like he was gripping it, but he had a bag covering his whole head. And also, I've seen a lot of dead folk through my coroner work, and I swear, I believe this fellow was dead as stone. . . ."

Belle put on a smile and stepped toward Brand. "Let me see what I can do to put your mind onto something different. How much have you had to drink, anyway, seeing images of dead men with sacks over their heads riding down the middle of a street with a storm coming on?"

Brand looked past her again, and shook his head. "No. I believe I've changed my mind. Here . . . I'll give you some money anyway, for your time. I got to go see what that was. I'm sorry." He dug a small bit of cash from a pocket and tossed it toward her, then headed at a near run up the alley toward the street.

Brand reached the street just as lightning filled it with light. A few drops of rain pattered down, big, thick drops that hit the earth with a dull *splat*.

There it was, down the street a short distance . . . the wagon with the two men aboard. As he trotted in that direction, Brand kept his eye on the man on the rider's side of the wagon bench. No sign of movement he could see, even when the rain heightened a bit.

As the rain picked up, the wagon's driver steered toward a space beneath an expansive overhanging balcony where he and his silent companion could escape the rain. Brand hesitated, loath to intrude himself with a stranger, but his curiosity was so strong as to drive him on. He approached the wagon from the rear, then deliberately coughed to alert the driver of his presence.

Nick Anubis looked across his shoulder and saw Brand. "Good evening, sir," Anubis said. "Is this your dry space we've intruded into?"

"No, sir, not at all. Devilish bad weather, eh?" Brand replied, coming forward and putting out his hand for Anubis to shake. As he shook the Gypsy's hand, Brand found himself able to get a clearer view of the figure at his side, and to read the sign in the figure's lap.

"Good Lord, sir, is that in fact the infamous Tennessee Kid?"

Anubis grinned. "Well, sir, that is what the sign says. And indeed it is."

"How would you come to be riding down the street in Wiles, Kansas, in the dark with a storm building, with a dead outlaw by your side? And why is that cloth over his head?"

"Well, sir," replied Anubis, "I am riding with my friend Tennessee here for the very purpose of attracting attention just like what you are giving us. The weather is just an unplanned interference. I am part of a traveling exhibition . . . I should say, me and my dead outlaw friend here are both part of a traveling exhibition . . . one that is parked at the side track back yonder way, outside of town. The Outlaw Train, we call it."

" 'We,' you say . . . I have to doubt, sir, that your dead friend there calls your 'Outlaw Train' by any name at all." Brand chuckled at his own joke.

"You are right about that. The 'we' I referred to is me and my professional associate, the founder of the exhibition. The principal in our business is the man who conceived the whole idea in the first place and collected the first exhibits . . . Percival Raintree. Quite a planner, quite a natural showman. He ran the show by himself until he brought me in to provide my special expertise toward the cause."

"What is that expertise, sir, if I might ask? Stirring up attention by hauling a corpse through town?"

"Much more than that, Mr. . . ."

"Brand. Wilton Brand. Wiles County coroner."

"Nicholas Anubis. Good to meet you," the other said, putting out his hand for another shake. "Did you say county coroner?"

"I did."

"An embalmer as well, maybe?"

"I'm not, though I had a little training in it. Never practiced it, though. Why do you ask?"

"That's my line of work. That's what I do for the Outlaw Train. I embalm dead outlaws. Embalm them to last. Forever, pretty much."

Brand frowned, suddenly thoughtful. "I just noticed something there, Mr. Anubis—the Tennessee Kid here has only one leg."

"That's right. Chopped off by a half-wit while Tennessee was holed up in a house having his final standoff."

"What about his face? Why is it covered? I asked you already and you didn't say."

"Mr. Brand, you should learn your outlaw lore a little better. You need to pay a visit to the Outlaw Train and let us educate you. The Tennessee Kid's head is covered up because his face isn't there anymore. It was shot off by a Texas Ranger with a shotgun. You, being a coroner, can stand to see such as that, just like I can. The public, though, they don't take well to such gruesomeness."

"May I . . ."

Anubis glanced around. Rain was falling harder now and the wind was still rising. No one on the street he could see. "Come on around to the other side."

"Good Lord!" Brand exclaimed when Anubis lifted the mask. "I've seen damaged flesh before, but that's the worst of it!"

Anubis nodded. "Yes, sir. Tennessee here took quite a bit of damage when that Ranger gave him the old lead shot. Quite a bit of damage." He lowered the cloth.

"Wait . . . there's something I want to see closer," said Brand.

"Suit yourself." Again the cloth went up.

Brand put a foot on the wagon and hefted himself up, drawing close to the ruin that was the Tennessee Kid's shotgunned face. Anubis was surprised; typically, on the rare occasions members of the public had seen what was under the cloth mask, the impulse had been to flee in horror, not draw closer. Anubis was further surprised when he saw Brand's nostrils flaring. The man was sniffing the embalmed flesh. And then, Brand reached up and touched it, pushing against the exposed meat.

"Mr. Brand, what are you doing?" Anubis asked.

"Mr. Anubis, sir, this is remarkable," Brand said. "I've seen embalming of this sort, firsthand, only once before."

"You've seen it before?"

"Yes."

"Mummy in a museum?"

"Well, yes, but one other time, much more recently. There was a human leg, severed, found lying beside the railroad tracks east of town. That leg was mummified, and bore precisely the same chemical odor I detect in the flesh of this similarly embalmed figure here. A figure that, I must note, has only one leg."

Anubis was at a loss for words. He looked fearful for a few moments. Brand read his expression.

"How recently did you come by the corpse of the Tennessee Kid, sir?" Brand asked.

"Er . . . quite recently, sir. Quite recently."

"Then how did he come to be embalmed? The Tennessee Kid died upwards of two years ago, as I recall it. But clearly this corpse shows almost no sign of pre-embalming decay. If you obtained the body 'quite recently,' who did this remarkable job of preservation?"

"It was . . . I . . . Sir, why are you questioning me so closely? I feel like a witness in a court of law."

"Mr. Anubis, may I ask you a question straight out?"

"Go ahead. Shoot." While he spoke, Anubis put the hood back in place on the Tennessee Kid's head.

"I have a theory, and I wish to ask you if this is correct. And I ask you in advance to take no offense, despite the fact my theory, if true, falsifies the story you have already presented."

"It won't be the first time I've been called a liar, sir. When you work in a showman's trade, there are plenty who question every word out of your mouth."

"Well, sir, here, then, is my theory. I believe that you did embalm this corpse, as you said. And I believe you have done so with a level of skill and technique that is perhaps otherwise unknown in the embalming profession."

"Thank you."

"But I also believe, sir, that this is not in fact the corpse of the Tennessee Kid. If it is the Tennessee Kid, it cannot be true that you preserved his remains 'quite recently.' It simply cannot be, given the date of the Tennessee Kid's death."

"What are you saying, sir?"

"I'm saying that I believe you are involved in a typical showman's deception. I believe you obtained a body of some individual, embalmed that body 'quite recently,' to use your own phrase, and after that process was complete, decided—in consultation with your partner, no doubt—to transform the body into that of the infamous Tennessee Kid, so you could display it as such, for profit. So you shotgunned the face and amputated the leg, and disposed of the latter by throwing it off your 'Outlaw Train' while it was en route to Wiles."

Anubis looked like a cornered rabbit. But he cleared his throat and quickly gained composure. "You are an imaginative man, Mr. Brand. After only minutes of conversation you have constructed an elaborate scenario explaining my involvement in a situation about which I know nothing. I'm not in the habit of dumping severed legs off moving trains, sir."

"Well, it's a mighty big coincidence, that leg turning up, preserved just like that body sitting beside you there, and you and your train in the county just at that same time."

"Well, there's some other explanation, my friend. I may not know that explanation, but I am sure there is one. Because I know nothing about that leg."

But Brand was not listening. His attention had been caught by the sight of the beautiful Katrina Haus walking hurriedly down the boardwalk on the far side of the street. She was taking the full brunt of the rain, hair stringing down across her shoulders and the fabric of her tight-fitting dress clinging to her shapely torso.

Suddenly Anubis and the Tennessee Kid were no longer of interest. Without another word Brand left the sheltered area and splashed across the muddy street toward Katrina's swift-moving form.

Just then the wind buffeted him, sweeping down the street from west to east. This was no ordinary wind, though; it was so strong as to nearly knock

Brand off his feet. He lost his hat and saw it sail down the street, ten feet off the ground, until out of sight. When he turned again, Katrina Haus was climbing to her feet, holding to a nearby hitch post to keep her balance in the wind. She had been knocked off her feet by the powerful gust.

"Are you all right, Miss Haus?" Brand called over the howl of the wind.

Katrina seemed disoriented. Brand wondered if she'd struck her head on the hitch post when she fell.

"I'm . . . I'm fine, sir," she said. Just then another, weaker, gust struck, and Brand saw what appeared to be an envelope blow out of her hand and dance down the wind as his hat had done.

"Shall I chase that down for you, ma'am?" Brand offered.

"No need, sir. But thank you. I doubt it can be found now. This wind is remarkably strong!"

"I've lived here long enough to know that such weather as this can lead to—" Lightning flared, a long flash that filled the roiling sky with brilliance like a bright noon.

Bess Keely marveled at the scarcity of saloons in this town. Not at all typical for a Western town. But at length she located the Redskin Princess, from whence Sheriff Crowe had been blasted off the mortal coil, and there purchased a cheap bottle of whiskey. She could not know, of course, that she was procuring for Dewitt Stamps a life-ruining poison up until his reformation . . . a poison of which he was now ready to partake again, despite years of stubborn resistance and sacred vows to the contrary.

Bess was a woman of the outdoors by habit, and had trained herself to be attuned to the weather without much overt concentration upon it. Her instinct told her that the storm coming this night would be significant, perhaps unusually so.

She pulled her hat low against the rain and wind and pushed on up the street, back toward the jail with Dewitt's bottle tucked under her arm. She noticed a few other people moving about despite the storm—a very pretty young woman in a pale blue dress, who happened to fall when a strong burst of wind threw her off balance and at the same time yanked something out of her hand and blew it down the street.

Then Bess noticed something else: a wagon parked under a sheltering cover on the opposite side of the street. Two men sat on the seat bench, one moving around restlessly, the other still as a statue and holding a sign. And wearing a hood that covered his entire head. Very strange.

Stranger yet was the inner disturbance that the unmoving figure caused when she looked at him. Even though she could see nothing beneath the hood, she had an uncanny feeling of somehow knowing this man. It was unaccountable.

Bess found herself drawn toward that wagon. She crossed the street, nearly falling herself in the strong and rising wind, and almost dropping Dewitt's bottle. The driver of the wagon noticed her as she came close, and greeted her, as most did on first glance, as "sir."

"I'm no 'sir,'" she said. "But never mind it. I'm curious about who that is beside you."

"This is none other than the famous and departed Tennessee Kid," Anubis replied. "His face is covered because of the gruesome manner of his death."

Bess opened her mouth to request that the hood be removed, but the issue was rendered moot when a new jolt of wind caught the hood and tore it off the dead man's head. It blew away and Bess gasped at the terrible sight of the shotgun-ruined face.

Yet something drew her around the wagon to the other side, where the dead man was perched. She had to look more closely at the meaty remains of that face, hideous though it was.

Anubis seemed embarrassed by the exposure of the destroyed face, and actually tried to cover it with his hand, then his hat. No matter. Bess hiked herself up on the side of the wagon and looked closely at the dead man's right ear, and the area just behind it.

"Good God!" she whispered.

"I know, ma'am," Anubis said. "It is a horrible vision to see. That's why we keep it covered. Damn this wind. . . ."

Bess shook her head vigorously. "No . . . no. That's not what I'm reacting to. Mister, this dead man beside you, I know him. I know him by the scarring around his ear . . . that's scarring that resulted from him being attacked by a biting dog when he was only six years old. Almost tore his ear off, that dog did. And left him with very distinctive scars that stayed with him for good."

"What are you talking about, ma'am?"

"This man isn't any 'Tennessee Kid,' sir. This man is Ben Keely. My brother."

Anubis's mouth worked like that of a dying fish out of water, gasping vainly.

Bess Keely drew the Remington pistol she carried in a holster on her right hip, and leveled it at Anubis. "Is your name Raintree, mister?"

At that moment, from the railed platform in the open portion of the steeple of the Methodist church a little down the street, a boyish voice pierced through the howl of the wind.

"Twister!" Oliver Wicks, the climbing boy, called down. "Off to the west! Big one, and coming this way!"

CHAPTER NINETEEN

Oliver Wicks clung to the platform rail, fighting the wind's efforts to tear him away, and watched the monstrous, twisting funnel tear its way across the landscape. He could see almost nothing of it except in those moments lightning allowed it, but each new jolt of light revealed that the spinning finger of Satan was moving closer.

For the first time in his life Oliver felt afraid to be where he was, clinging like an ant to a high place. He was a confident boy, secure in his practiced abilities to move squirrel-like through the heights with little danger of falling . . . but his confidence faded in the face of the oncoming cyclone. Yet he made no move to descend; he was frozen, paralyzed by terror. All he could do was cling and watch and call out his warning to the town below, and pray that before it reached him, the twister would either die away of its own accord or leap over the area where he was.

The former option didn't seem likely. The twister seemed to be growing stronger and larger, not diminishing. Oliver ceased his warning shouts; the wind was so strong now as to blow away his words like feeble straws, and the roar was louder than anything the boy had ever heard. Oliver held fast to the railing and prayed hard that he would go to heaven when the twister got him, for he was sure now that it would. It was something he just knew.

A couple of streets over, another person watched the coming tornado from a high perch and began to anticipate his own death just as Oliver was. Simon Montague's old eyes were feeble, but the lightning was so bright that even he could see with clarity what it illuminated . . . and what he saw was a black, moving, spinning wall that seemed intent upon reaching and striking the town of Wiles. The old man's spit-dribbled lips moved in a silent prayer and he backed away from the window that provided his only accessible view of the world outside. The glass of the window was rattling hard in its frame, ready to break out under the buffeting air.

The old man moved back toward his chair, but stumbled and went down hard on his knees. He grunted at the impact of kneecaps on floor, but managed not to fall completely over. He groped at and found the chair he'd been attempting to reach, and used it to prop himself up.

"Lord God, forgive my sins and take me to your glory," he said. "My time has come to die, and I am ready. Forgive me, Lord, for my transgressions—"

His further words were cut off by an explosive, shattering, splintering burst, a noise filling his ears like the roar of cannon, as the front wall of the emporium, struck by the hard winds moving in advance of the tornado funnel, ripped away and flew like a gigantic, mad bird across the rooftops of Wiles, Kansas.

The old man felt his feeble body being lifted by the incredibly powerful air and pulled toward the vacant space that had previously been filled by the front wall of his secret residence. Desperately he put his hands out and randomly found a hold on an upright beam. A half second's decline in the wind's force allowed him time to wrap his arms around that beam and clasp his hands together on its far side in an embrace of life.

Simon Montague expected to die, but he would not be pulled to his doom without a fight.

Katrina Haus wished she had not left the hotel. Perhaps she would have been equally unsafe there as she was here on the street, but at least she would have walls around her and not be exposed directly to the stinging wind and bulletlike rain.

She had left the hotel in order to fulfill the request on Howard Ashworth's card, to meet him at the specified time near the emporium. Of course, at the time he'd written that request he had certainly not been expecting such weather as this. If he could have seen this coming, Katrina knew, he would have asked to meet her at a different time, and certainly at a different place, not in an open lot on the edge of town.

The weather had already been bad when Katrina left the hotel, but it had degraded much further and faster than she had anticipated as she walked across town. But she'd always been that sort who, once she had set her course or her plan, was not prone to deviate. If Howard Ashworth wanted to meet her tonight, she would meet him. Unpleasant, plain man that he was, he was also a man of means, and was willing to pay well for what she provided him. Katrina had known many men such as Ashworth in her day, men whose wives had grown old and harsh and unloving. Men to whom a young beauty such as she was could hardly be resisted.

Finding a momentary refuge in an alley, where the rain was lessened and the wind deflected, she caught her breath and made herself think through her situation. Why should she go on? At this point, no one would be waiting for her in any open lot near the emporium. The storm had seen to that. Not even alley cats and skunks would undertake coition in this weather.

But perhaps Ashworth would be nearby, in some shed or barn or other shelter, watching for her. And if the storm lessened, she and he could have their rendezvous, she could collect her money for services rendered, and the evening would not be wasted.

Then she remembered the warning given her by Jimmy Wills back at the hotel. What if he proved right, and it wasn't Howard Ashworth seeking to meet her at all, but Howard's wife? Maybe the woman had learned somehow of her husband's carnal tryst with the beautiful traveling prostitute. Maybe she had in mind a bit of vengeful repayment.

Katrina vowed to herself to be wary and ready, then began moving down the alley. She reached Emporium Street just as the wind doubled and tripled its intensity, and watched in shock as the upper front of the big building tore away and twisted off in the stout wind almost as easily as had that piece of paper that had blown from her hand.

A stray and splintering board torn free from a shed at the end of the street struck Katrina in the side of the head and send her flailing to the dirt. Groaning, she managed to reach up and touch the tender and bleeding fresh wound on the side of her head before she passed out.

The huge twister entering the town made a sudden change, rising into the clouds and skipping over the rest of the town. Over in his church steeple, Oliver Wicks breathed a prayer of thanks that he had managed to hang on to his perch. Mere moments before it had looked as though the cyclone was going to strike the church directly.

Oliver's sense of relief did not last long. Looking back out across the plains and low, rolling terrain west of town, he saw that another twister was forming, this one perhaps larger even than the one that had just spared him, and most of the town.

Time to descend. Even for a climbing boy who was at home in high places, the ground was sometimes the best place to be. There was a ditch beside one of the back alleys, and that, Oliver decided, was where he needed to place himself.

By the time Oliver had reached that ditch and thrown himself down in it, trying to ignore the water running beneath and around him, Katrina Haus was coming to and slowly pushing herself to her feet. Woozy and unfocused, she staggered to the left, her feet getting caught up in the hem of her dress and tripping her. She went down again, bumping her shoulder against the base of a telegraph pole.

She did not pass out again, but felt astonishingly weak.

She lost all ambition to meet Howard Ashworth in the designated lot near the emporium. The mere thought of trying to endure an encounter with a man while she felt this unstable was enough to sicken her. Yet she moved forward is if she had a clear destination. It was all done unthinkingly by this point; her only focused desire now was to find a place that was safe from the storm.

Yet she had just seen a portion of the biggest and strongest building in town ripped apart as if it were made of twigs. Where could she go? Was there any safe place at all in this town at the moment?

She looked up at the ruptured and gaping front of the emporium and saw something that brought her to a stop despite the driving rain in her face. An old man, bearded, was clinging in obvious fright to a support beam in what remained of the emporium attic. Wiping rain and grit from her eyes, Katrina looked at the man and decided she had never seen him before. He reminded her of Campbell Montague, but Campbell had no beard and did not seem as feeble as this man.

Lightning flashed and bathed the entire scene in bright light, and she knew he saw her as clearly as she saw him. He stared hard at her. Then darkness filled the street again, and when the next lightning flash came, she was no longer there, and Simon Montague could not see where she had gone.

At that moment Simon realized how exposed he was. He'd managed to hide from the world up here, behind the wall that was now a gaping hole, but there was no hiding to be done now. All he could do now was hope that the building continued to stand until he could get out of it, and that no other funnel clouds would come ripping through to suck him out of the gutted attic portion.

"Uncle Simon!"

The call came from Macky, who appeared at the largely undamaged rear section of Simon's attic, having climbed the private stairs from below. Macky came up and put his arm around his uncle's stooped shoulders and looked with concern at his face.

"I'm fine, Macky, fine," Simon said. "What about you?"

"There was, there was a big, huge thing, twisting all around, turning and blowing and roaring so *loud!*"

"It was a twister, Macky. A cyclone. They happen sometimes in this part of the country. Did it hurt you?"

"No . . . scared me. Scared me bad. It hurt the store, Uncle Simon. It tore off your wall, and now, if people look up here, they can see you're here. Won't be secret no more."

"It won't matter, Macky. People aren't going to care about such things for a while, not with the weather this dangerous."

Macky held to his uncle, shivering in fright. He stared out the open front of the emporium as though he expected to see Satan rise from the street below and float in to consume them like a great beast. The rain and wind continued, not at tornado force at the moment, but touched with a chill and somehow bitter on the lips and tongue.

"Macky, there was a woman in the street below, a young woman, very pretty. Nobody I had seen out the window before. Then she moved away and was gone. Do you know who it might have been?"

"It might have been my friend, Miss Haus. She's a real pretty lady, and nice. She told me I could be her friend."

"Why is she in town?"

"She talks to dead people, Uncle. They tell her things and she tells their kinfolk."

"Don't believe in such things, Macky. That's not real. That's not the way the world really works."

The wind began to rise again suddenly, and from the west came a renewed roaring that seemed, as before, to be coming toward the town. "We should get down from here, Uncle Simon," Macky said. "It might blow down the rest of the store with us in it."

The old man loathed the thought of leaving what had been his refuge for a good while now, the place he could hide from a harsh and judgmental world. But he knew Macky was right. The upper reaches of an already damaged and weakened building were not where to be when a tornado was sweeping in.

Time to descend to the street before the next twister arrived.

"Let's go, Macky," the old man said.

They descended. Exiting the building into an alley, they were buffeted by the harsh weather and Simon found himself unsure where to go. After a few moments of indecision, during which the approaching roar grew much louder, they headed toward the rear of the alley and into a nearby lot filled with brush and wild grass. A couple of rough sheds stood around the rear perimeter. They went to the closest one.

Inside, they stood in shock and looked down at what lay in the middle of the dirt floor. The old man shook his head. "The storm killed her somehow. Something hitting her in the head, I suppose."

Macky, though, knelt and examined the corpse of Katrina Haus more closely. He opened his mouth as if to point out something, then seemingly changed his mind and stood again without a word.

Even if he had spoken, he would not have been heard. The sound of a second twister hitting the remnant of the Montague Emporium, and the sound of the building exploding, was so loud and intense that anything Macky might have said would have been masked and lost.

He and his uncle crouched together beside the body of the most beautiful woman ever to pass through Wiles, Kansas, and clung to each other, both wondering if they would survive, if their kinsman Campbell Montague had survived the storm, or would, and what would become of the town of Wiles when at last this horrible night was over.

Macky closed his eyes tightly, unwilling to be looking in case the twister struck the shed that sheltered them, or in case some heavy piece of the shattered emporium came falling through the shed roof. He prayed for safety, and while he did so, made a promise: *Lord, I'll tell Luke Cable about what I saw when I looked at Miss Haus. Because I think I know what it means, and he needs to know.*

CHAPTER TWENTY

"You've told me some of this story before, Father," said a man in his midtwenties to the older man beside him. "But I don't recall how it was you got free of that tree you were tied to."

"I owe that to a man who came along at just the right time," said Luke Cable to his son. They were standing on a boardwalk along Emporium Avenue in the town of Wiles, in a year early in a new century, more than two decades past the day two major twisters had devastated that Kansas town and turned the Montague Emporium into a huge pile of rubble. "In a way, you might be able to say that Scar Nolan had saved my life by tying me to that tree after he clonked me on the skull. That twister passed right over, and made splinters out of the Outlaw Train just yards from where I was, but being tied to that tree kept me from maybe getting blown off into the sky like a leaf. Nearly tore my arms out of my shoulder sockets, but probably kept me alive, too."

"But how did you get loose after the whirlwinds had blown over?"

"I've got a traveling journalist to thank for that. Man by the last name of Baum who had come to Wiles to find Percival Raintree and his Outlaw

Train. Like most everybody else in town that day, Baum got surprised by the weather. He picked just the wrong time to rent a horse and ride out to the Outlaw Train, but it's lucky for me he did. He saw me there on the ground, still tied to that tree, not even back to consciousness yet. He came over and cut me free, and it was about that time I woke up."

"Did Baum put you in his newspaper?"

"Ha! That man didn't work for any newspaper, not like you'd think of a newspaper. He wrote stories about ghosts and spooks and the like for a journal magazine, the *Argus* of something or other. He wrote a story up that said the Outlaw Train had been destroyed by a demon conjured up by Scar Nolan, who was angry about Raintree having a display related to one of his brothers. He mentioned me in his story by my title, but not by name, which suited me. There was some truth in the account he published, but not much. Nolan, sure enough, was angry about what was in the Outlaw Train, I suspect, but there wasn't any demon-conjuring involved in what he did about it. No demon other than Nolan himself, anyway."

"He shot Raintree?"

"Blew his brains all over the inside of that display car. There was just enough of it left to figure out what had happened."

The younger man looked across the street, where a large church reached skyward. "So that's where the emporium stood, is it?"

"That's the spot. It was a sight to see, that store. Bigger even than that Baptist church house there. When the twister took it down, it ruined poor old

Campbell Montague, though. Made him a sad and withdrawn kind of man. He built another store to replace it, just a small one, still standing over on that corner there. See? But he sold it off within a year of building it, and pretty much just hid himself away, almost like his brother Simon had done up in the attic of the original store. Funny twist in all that. Simon finally came out and joined the world again, and his brother turned hermit, doing nothing but hiding away and taking care of Macky as long as Macky lived. Campbell himself died the year after Macky was killed."

"How'd Macky get killed?"

"Macky was a good boy, but he was simple and he was careless. He walked out one day and got hit by a wagon that somebody was driving too fast around a corner. He's buried over in the town cemetery. Let's walk over that way and I'll show you his grave. And some others."

Luke and his son strode down the street, Luke examining the town he served as marshal a quarter century earlier. It had changed dramatically, but much of what he had known so well remained, too.

The cemetery held the past. Luke took off his hat and walked solemnly between the stones, reading names, pointing out in particular the resting places of Macky and Campbell Montague. Moving on, he came to a small marker. His son joined him and they read the name together in silence.

"Was she really as beautiful as you say, Father?"

Luke glanced around, making sure his wife wasn't near. The former Sally James of Ellsworth, who had married Luke in 1879, had gone earlier to visit the local dress shop, leaving her husband and son to take a walk around the town Luke had not visited since the spring of 1880, the year he'd left Kansas and moved to Missouri to take up a new career as a house carpenter.

"To speak truthfully, Katrina Haus was probably the most beautiful woman I've seen in sixty-three years of life," Luke said. "You needn't mention to your mother that I said that."

"Is that why you looked around before you answered?"

"No point in stirring up trouble you don't have need for," Luke replied with a quick grin. "A man should never say within hearing of his wife that there is, or even ever was, a woman more beautiful. Though in the case of Katrina Haus, I don't know there was ever a greater beauty than she was, here or anywhere else."

The younger man looked down at the grave. "It's a shame such a beauty should be killed by a cyclone, of all things."

Luke shook his head. "It wasn't a cyclone that killed her, son. Far from it. It was . . . murder."

"She was murdered?"

"She was."

"Are you the one who figured it out?"

Luke chuckled mirthlessly. "No, son. No. The only thing I figured out in the whole situation was that I had neither the skill nor the real desire to be a peace officer anymore. It was Katrina Haus, in her death, who caused me to come to that conclusion. Her, and Ben Keely, considering what happened to him."

"So who determined Katrina was murdered?"

"The half-wit nephew of Campbell Montague. Macky."

"A half-wit figured that out?"

"He did. It was Macky and Simon Montague who found her body after they fled the emporium during the storm. She was lying on her back in a shed, mouth open just a little. Macky got close enough to notice something visible near the roof of her mouth."

"What was it?"

"The head of a pin. A kind of French hat pin they sold in the emporium. Big, long hat pins."

"I don't understand what you're getting at, Father."

Luke looked at his son. "A hat pin had been thrust through the roof of her mouth. All the way up through her head into her brain. I know it for a fact because I saw it myself as me and Wilton Brand examined the corpse before she was buried. Wilton found evidence that the pin had been pushed in several times, pulled out and pushed in again and again, you see. To make sure her brain was punctured enough to ensure she was dead."

"Why did the murderer leave it in the last time? Tiny little holes in the roof of her mouth probably wouldn't have been noticed by themselves."

"I think she was frightened away, maybe by the first hit of the twister at the emporium, which was close by, or maybe even by the approach of Simon and Macky after they fled the store building."

" 'She,' you said?"

"Come over here."

Luke led the way to a different grave. "Here's your murderess, in my opinion."

The gravestone bore the name of Clara Ashworth.

"I did some asking around after the fact and found out from Jimmy Wills, who at the time was just a young fellow working as hotel clerk, that Katrina Haus had received a note at the hotel, on stock imprinted with Howard Ashworth's name, Howard being Clara's husband, asking Katrina to meet Howard in that same lot near the emporium that Simon and Macky ended up fleeing to. But Jimmy told me that handwriting on the note looked more like Clara had written it than Howard, though Howard's name was signed at the bottom."

"Why would she do that?"

"I think Clara had figured out that her husband had been unfaithful to her. With Katrina Haus. Maybe Howard had even confessed it to her, I don't know. I think it was Clara's revenge. The woman was so proud she couldn't bear the idea of her husband making a fool of her by seeking out the affections of a common whore. So she contrived to lure Katrina to that empty lot and that dark shed, and kill her there. What she couldn't know at the time she left that note was that a tornado was going to sweep through at the same time she planned to meet Katrina Haus. My theory is that Katrina was either knocked out by the storm and pulled into that shed by Clara, and those pins thrust into her brain while she was senseless, or Clara maybe clouted her in the head with something and knocked her cold, then killed her."

"Yeah, she pretty much had to be unconscious to be killed that way. Nobody would lie there with their senses about them and let someone shove hat pins up through the roof of their mouth."

"Exactly. And by the way, Clara Ashworth was known to have bought a box of those hat pins at the emporium, just shortly before all these things happened."

"So was Clara ever charged with the murder?"

"Son, we found Clara Ashworth dead the day after the storm, caught under the rubble of a building that fell in the wind. I think that after she killed Katrina and fled that shed, she was caught by the storm while she was trying to get home. Wrong place at the wrong time, and crushed to death."

"Well, it saved having to have had a trial, I guess."

"Yes. And it saved me from any notion of wanting to continue as town marshal. Within a week of the storm coming through, I gave my resignation. Especially after I found that Ben certainly wouldn't be coming back. His sister had come into town, you see, in hope she'd find he was alive and well. And she found him, all right, but not alive and well. He'd been murdered in Kentucky by Percival Raintree, who wanted a criminal relic Ben possessed at that time, to put on his Outlaw Train. Raintree gunned Ben down out on a remote road in Kentucky. Shot him in the face with a shotgun. I reckon that was what gave Raintree the idea of hiding his crime by making poor old Ben into a relic himself. There was a criminal of that period of time, you see, who had been about Ben's size, and got killed by a similar shotgun blast to the face. The Tennessee Kid, they called him. So Raintree sneaked Ben's corpse onto his train and left Kentucky to resume touring in Missouri and Kansas. Had his partner, fellow name of Nicholas Anubis, preserve Ben's body and pass him off as the Tennessee Kid. Ben's corpse couldn't be recognized because there was nothing left of the face. And of course they kept the head covered up with a cloth, anyway. But apparently it took them some time to recollect that the real Tennessee Kid had also lost one leg, so they cut off one of Ben's legs and dumped it off the train while they were about to roll through Wiles to the old railroad side track out west of town. That was the last stop the Outlaw Train would ever make. The tornado saw to that. The tornado, and Scar Nolan, when he killed Raintree."

"What became of Anubis?"

"Killed in the same tornado. He'd come into town with the body of 'the Tennessee Kid,' and it was then that Bess Keely recognized the corpse of her brother. She identified him by way of some old dog-bite scars around one of Ben's ears. I remember those scars myself. They were the only identifying marks left on Ben's body after Raintree killed him in Kentucky."

"What became of Bess?"

"She went back to Kentucky. By train. Had Ben's body shipped back at the same time to be buried in the family plot. Otherwise, I guess he'd be buried in this cemetery here."

"Is Dewitt here?"

"Come over. I'll show you."

They walked to a grave in the far corner of the cemetery. The stone bore the words HERE LIES THE MORTAL REMAINS OF DEWITT ISAAC

STAMPS, b. 1840, d. 1896, CHILD OF GOD. WASHED CLEAN OF HIS SINS IN THE BLOOD OF THE LAMB.

"That's nice," Luke's son said.

"It is. First time I've seen this stone, even though I'm the one who wired in the money to pay for it. They did a good job. The words on it, Dewitt wrote himself when he got sick enough to know he wasn't going to survive."

"He was a good man, you've told me."

"One of the finest I've ever known. It's why I named my own son after him."

Dewitt Cable smiled. "I'm named after a town drunk. Kind of funny."

"I'll bet Dewitt himself found it funny, when I wrote to tell him about it. He was a humble man. But he was sure no town drunk when he died, no matter what he'd been years and years before. He had only one occasion of backsliding in his life, to my knowledge. The night the storm hit, Bess Keely had gone down to the saloon and bought Dewitt a bottle of whiskey. He'd managed to persuade himself that it was all right for him to have a little drink. But like so many who get trapped by the bottle, Dewitt learned he couldn't stop with just a 'little drink.' He got drunk on that whiskey Bess bought him, and it was months before he was dry and clean again. But after that, Ben never faltered again. Became a preacher, preaching mostly to men who had been like he was, and giving them help. There's a lot of men alive today who would have been dead by alcohol if not for Dewitt Stamps. You can bear his name with pride, son."

"I will. And I do." Dewitt Cable turned to his father. "I'm glad you decided to come back and visit this town. And I'm glad you let me come with you."

Luke grinned. "Me, too, son. Hey, I see your mother coming across the street there, heading this way. Go on to her so she'll know she's found us."

The younger man obeyed, leaving Luke alone at the gravestone. He looked down and read its words one more time.

"I'll be seeing you later on, Dewitt," he said. "Until then, you rest in peace. Hear? I love you, Dewitt. Admired you more than you ever knew."

Luke Cable put his hat back on his head and walked off to rejoin his family. When he reached them, his son had one more question for him.

"Father, did Katrina Haus wind up to actually be . . . what was her name?"

"Kate Bender? I asked Simon Montague that question, straight out. He'd seen Katrina clearly after she died, you remember, in that shed. He said her face was not that of Kate Bender. And he would have known. Katrina Haus was just a young woman who defrauded gullible people and used herself in wrong ways. But she was no murderer. No Kate Bender. No Clara Ashworth."

The Cable family walked together a few minutes without speaking. Then Luke said, "I noticed coming through town that the Taylor Café is still open, after all these years. Let's go have a meal, shall we?"

Sally Cable entwined her arm with her husband's and they made their way into the heart of Wiles, Kansas, together.

✂ ☐ **YES!**

Sign me up for the Leisure Western Book Club and send my FREE BOOKS! If I choose to stay in the club, I will pay only $14.00* each month, a savings of $9.96!

NAME: _____

ADDRESS: _____

TELEPHONE: _____

EMAIL: _____

☐ I want to pay by credit card.

☐ **VISA**　　☐ **MasterCard.**　　☐ **DISCOVER**

ACCOUNT #: _____

EXPIRATION DATE: _____

SIGNATURE: _____

Mail this page along with $2.00 shipping and handling to:
Leisure Western Book Club
PO Box 6640
Wayne, PA 19087
Or fax (must include credit card information) to:
610-995-9274
You can also sign up online at **www.dorchesterpub.com**.
*Plus $2.00 for shipping. Offer open to residents of the U.S. and Canada only.
Canadian residents please call 1-800-481-9191 for pricing information.
If under 18, a parent or guardian must sign. Terms, prices and conditions subject to change. Subscription subject to acceptance. Dorchester Publishing reserves the right to reject any order or cancel any subscription.